ADMIRAL WRIGHT'S
HER⊙ICAL
STORICALS

DANIEL BOONE
and the
BATTLE *of* BOONESBOROUGH

ANNIE WINSTON

www.sonshipkidsbooks.com
www.heroicalstoricals.com

WHAT LEADERS ARE SAYING

"Be prepared for a whimsical moral journey that will excite even the least historical sorts."

–Sharon Wigal PhD
University of California, Irvine

"Annie Winston has a wonderful way of weaving in character lessons as she tells the stories of great historical heroes."

–Rosie Avila
Orange County Youth Commission

"Surely elementary school teachers throughout America will discover that Heroical Storicals do provide the spark that can bring enthusiastic reading and class discussion on what it means to think clearly and act right. One educator commented, 'I can use your book as a basis for providing a values based program which my students desperately need.'"

–Russell Williams
President of PassKeys Foundation

WHAT KIDS ARE SAYING

"I love your book. Every kid should read it."

—*Danny*

"*Heroical Storicals* is my favorite book. It makes history fun and interesting."

—*Lauren*

"*Heroical Storicals* has a newness to it that you don't usually find in a book. History comes alive and I couldn't put *Heroical Storicals* down."

—*Brian*

"Heroical Storicals ranks higher than most of the other books I have read."

—*Jacob*

"Heroical Storicals was so good and it was really funny!"

—*Noa*

ADMIRAL WRIGHT'S
HER◉ICAL
STORICALS

ISBN: 978-0-9779535-4-7   Third Edition
Visit: www.21stcenturypress.com
Cover art © 2004 Mark Fredrickson
Cover design by Lee Fredrickson
Cover © 2007 by Sonship Press
Inside Illustrations: Keith Locke
Book Design: Lee Fredrickson & Terry White

SONSHIP
PRESS

Special Dedication

A special dedication goes to all the curious students in the world who desire truth and understanding. My sincerest hope is that everyone who reads Heroical Storicals will always be the 'curious student' who is forever learning and growing and never ... ever... ever... arriving. In the words of the Admiral, whom you shall soon meet in the following pages, *"If you are not learning and growing, then what are you doing?"*

Noted Mates

I am very grateful for the prayers of family, friends and supporters who have encouraged me to stay the course despite obstacles that at times were overwhelming. Such support will not be forgotten. Thank you! Marina Ball, Marion Brumfield, Hart Crary, Dana DiCiano, Mojgan Firoozi, Lisa Gluck, Jim and Jocylyn Hahn, Ron Legnon, Stepfanie Meurer, David Ochi, Dave Salo, Diane Schlesinger, Bob and Marie Schlesinger, Daisy Stacy, Ryan Tai, Carol Timmons, Steve Turbow, Andrew and Marilyn Yu.

A special thank you goes to Lee Fredrickson, my publisher, who allowed me to become a published author. I appreciate his vision for seeing *Heroical Storicals* as a unique book for a unique time.

A special thank you also goes to my first editor. Your help was timely and indispensable and it will always be remembered and appreciated.

Another thank you goes to my identical twin sister, Vanessa Browne and her children, Jessica and James. Without your early morning phone call sixteen years ago voicing your concern over the lack of positive role models for children, *Heroical Storicals* may have never been born.

And a very special thank you goes to my three children, Amy, Emily and Matthew.

Finally and most importantly, a very special thanks goes to my Creator, who gave me the wisdom, courage and strength to write Heroical Storicals. He truly deserves the praise, glory and honor.

Ship's Log

Chapter One

A Spinning Compass

Willie Venturely was not just an ordinary boy, but also a very adventurous boy, who didn't like Miss Dullywinkle's fifth-grade history class because historical heroes were talked and read about as if they were the most important characters in the world. Poor Willie couldn't muster up one little bit of interest or curiosity for history or heroes, not even a teeny-weeny amount, no matter how hard he tried. All he wanted to do was climb trees, race down hills on his bike, find collectibles that he secretly stashed in his desk at school, dream of adventure and avoid his twin sister, Tillie, whenever possible.

Today, like every other day at school, Willie sat in his chair ready to fish—not in a pond, but in his very cluttered desk. The backside of his palm was arched up at the entrance while he waited with great expectation and eagerness to begin. Such eager expectation for today's fishing came about because Willie had found a new treasure which he happened to trip over while running late to school that morning. He was late because he had returned home to get his raincoat after his twin sister had scolded him about the matter. On his way back to school he had stumbled on a strange some-thing and almost landed facedown in a mud puddle. Amazingly, Willie managed to miss the mud puddle by one very small inch, though his right hand didn't miss landing on the strange something, a most unusual compass. The compass was unusual because it was warm to the touch, almost hot, even though the morning was cool, with dreary skies and dark clouds. Willie felt good holding the unusual compass in his hand. He couldn't wait to examine it more closely when he had more time. Willie glanced at his watch and let out a small moan. He was going to be late again. He shoved the compass in his pants pocket and ran to school.

Willie slipped into the classroom without anyone noticing except Tillie, who gave him one of her worst frowns. He hurriedly stuffed the compass as far as he could inside his desk with all his other treasures. Willie knew that he would have to wait before he could safely search for it. He had learned from experience that he dare not begin to fish for his new treasure until Miss Dullywinkle was distracted enough.

Every day Miss Dullywinkle read aloud

from encyclopedias about different characters from history. No student (no matter how clever) could completely escape the very long and very dull readings. Some students fell asleep, but Willie came the closest to escaping because he went fishing in his desk. It was only during Miss Dullywinkle's readings that Willie could safely fish without fear of being seen by the keen eye of his teacher. Even then, he could still be caught; she would have to be distracted even further. If Willie were caught, he would be forced to endure the awful Dullywinkle Doom: a cold, hard, shameful seat known as the dunce stool. (We'll learn more about this a little bit later.)

As Miss Dullywinkle continued her boring encyclopedic reading, Willie kept his gaze fixed on her, not wanting to miss the signal that it was completely safe to fish. The signal had not arrived, so Willie continued to act as if he was listening to her. No character from history, hero or not, ever interested Willie. Today's encyclopedic reading was extra boring. In fact, it was excruciatingly boring, which meant that it was so painful to listen to that Willie didn't end up listening to one word. Miss Dullywinkle was reading about some historical hero named Daniel Boone and the Battle of Boonesborough. Her words bounced off Willie's ears like flat rubber balls. But there was one word that never bounced off his ears: RESEARCH. At the sound of that word, a woozy queasy feeling came over Willie and he was left with an ache in his tummy. He felt sick because he knew that another trip to the library was going to happen soon, and then another report on a historical hero was going to be due!

For Willie, having to go to the library and do any kind of research was like eating spinach leaves splattered with the most horrible tasting mustard. He couldn't understand why anyone would like going to libraries and writing information on little white lined cards that were supposed to help straighten your thinking. It never worked for Willie. He usually ended up dropping his cards and then mixing them up, as well as making a mess. Willie usually got a stiff scolding from Mrs. Dexter, the librarian, who made it her duty to set students like him on the right path of discipline and order. It wasn't that Willie didn't like discipline and order, but he had a hard time making those qualities work for him. It didn't help that he was convinced that learning about dead heroes from a long time ago had no meaning for his life at Merriweather Bay.

Tillie looked over at her brother and glared, while silently mouthing the words, "Pay attention and stop trying to fish!" She knew about her brother's desk fishing and did not approve. Willie wasn't getting his homework and class work done and Tillie felt responsible. They were twins, and she didn't want to have a twin who was lazy. Tillie hated being compared to her brother, especially when other students came up and said, "How come your brother is always late and never turns in his homework on time? I thought you two were twins. Twins are supposed to be the same."

Willie and Tillie were not the same. Willie always pushed the boundaries of adventure and

fun—like the time he tried to climb a tree to count the number of eggs in a robin's nest and bumped a hornets' nest instead. He almost fell out of the tree as he tried to climb down as fast as he could to escape the angry swarm! Tillie never pushed boundaries. She thought of herself as always being very careful and prudent. Tillie tried to do everything she was told and was quite pleased to be known as "the twin who minds the rules," especially when it came to turning her reports in on time.

Willie didn't care much about minding rules, especially class rules like turning reports in on time. He didn't care about history or heroes because it was boring memorizing names, dates and places, and doing research reports on heroes he didn't want to know anything about. Instead of struggling with learning how to do real research, Willie had given up on the idea completely. He decided that he wouldn't try to think and write out his own ideas. He simply copied word for word, out of whatever book was easiest to find on the hero's life. After he was done copying, he felt a little bit dishonest but he really didn't know that he had committed plagiarism, the act of stealing another person's words and ideas without giving any credit to them.

It was a good thing that Willie had never been caught for this dishonest act, but he had been caught desk fishing a few times. He was punished in a most embarrassing way. Willie was made to face the Dullywinkle Doom, that miserable stool in the front corner of the class. He had to sit with his back to the class, which made him feel very foolish, and, to make the matter worse, Miss Dullywinkle insisted that Willie wear a ridiculous and humiliating cone-shaped hat with a rubber band chinstrap that was too tight and left an ugly impression under his chin after he took it off.

When Willie sat on the misery stool, he

thought about why learning about heroes and history in Miss Dullywinkle's class was such a mind-numbing exercise. Willie didn't have to think hard at all. He knew why. You'll recall that Miss Dullywinkle read aloud from out-of-date encyclopedias and books that no one in the class was interested in, except Tillie. What was most painful and humiliating was that his back became an open dartboard for wet spitballs and eye-popping stares from bored students. Mean Billy Bones, the class bully, always shot the wet spitballs. Willie also couldn't forget about the last time he sat on the miserable stool. That was the time when Billy Bones' biggest, nastiest and wettest spitball smacked him with lightning speed right on his left ear. Poor Willie's earlobe throbbed for hours! From that time on, Willie made up his mind that he would never ever sit on that most miserable stool again, and he never did. Willie quickly perfected his desk fishing skills so that no paper rustling could be heard while he maneuvered around his collectibles. Willie had become a Master Desk Fisher, which meant that Miss Dullywinkle wouldn't catch him again.

With his hand still poised at the entrance of his desk, Willie suddenly noticed what he had been waiting to see: the signal that it was safe to fish. The signal came when Miss Dullywinkle paused to pop a breath mint in her mouth. This was one of the few times she allowed herself a little treat: a Pillworth's Pepperminto Wintofrostimint. She kept them in a small case locked in her teacher desk drawer. Miss Dullywinkle would savor the special treat as she read and imagined the people and places about which she was reading. As she relished the fresh, cool sensation, her imagination stirred with images of famous battles, far-off places where strong and courageous men and women of history had lives filled with noble and heroic deeds. She became so wrapped up in her experience of historical excitement and sweet minty goodness that she forgot all about her students, most of whom were falling asleep and some even falling out of their chairs from boredom. She really didn't understand that most of her students didn't welcome such an approach to learning. Willie thought that Miss Dullywinkle was more interested in making the students obey class rules like sitting quietly and listening to her encyclopedic readings than trying to come up with interesting ways to help them learn history, or any other subject.

While Miss Dullywinkle enjoyed her mint, Willie knew she would be more than distracted enough not to notice his desk fishing activities. As she continued to dreadfully drone on about Daniel Boone and the Battle of Boonesborough, Willie's hand carefully and oh-so-quietly entered his desk. While desk fishing, Willie liked to imagine himself as being someone who was highly trained and on a secret mission to discover a mystery that would change the world. He paused to carefully observe Miss Dullywinkle; he didn't want to be caught. "Yes," he told himself, "she's still got the mint rolling around in her mouth." He could continue to fish safely.

Willie moved his fingers around his collectibles with extreme precision, avoiding noisemaking of any kind. He skillfully maneuvered around an arrowhead carved out of rock, a starfish, a robin's nest holding a broken shell, a blue peacock feather and a spotted turtle shell. Willie wasn't going to give up until he found the unusual compass. He stretched his smallest pinky to the farthest corner inside his desk and then, at last, he felt metal. Willie's heart beat faster, and his palms began to sweat. His hands started to shake as he slowly pulled out his best find of the month. Not only was the compass still hot, but its directional arrow was spinning wildly, bouncing out of control, from North to South, and East to West.

Willie tried to figure out what was wrong, but before he could think very much, his neck twitched, he felt a quick tug and he was nudged to turn and look out the class window. At first he saw nothing, only rain falling. Then a burst of lightning lit the sky and Willie saw it, a Shiny Shiny Silver Ship. It was fantastic and it was flying. He rubbed his eyes to make sure he wasn't daydreaming. Willie had never seen such a Shiny Shiny Silver Ship or anything else so incredibly splendid. The sails were made of richly embroidered cloth that had gold and silver threads running in every direction, leaving a shimmering crisscrossed pattern that made the billowing sails appear electric. The base of the ship, where it would have been wooden, was made up of the shiniest metallic silver imaginable—reflecting light from all directions. Willie's eyes widened and his jaw dropped as he stared at the unbelievable happenings. His eye caught an oddly misshapen crow's nest that rested on top of a long pole made of ivory. The nest was misshapen because it was very large and happened to be a very real bird's nest made of sticks and twigs. In the nest sat a rain-drenched parrot, wearing a fishing hat that was too big for his head. The storm beaten parrot furiously flapped and struggled to leave its post to get out of the rain. Willie felt sorry for the bird. He wanted to fly out the window to help in some way.

The final bell rang, but Willie didn't hear it. All he heard was a loud, squeaky voice screeching in his ear. "What are you looking at? It's only raining out there. You should be listening to Miss Dullywinkle! The Daniel Boone research report is due tomorrow. Mine is done, and I know that yours is not!"

The loud, squeaky voice belonged to Tillie. She stood over him flipping her ponytail. She only did this when she felt a bit better than her brother, especially after trying to correct anything wrong or different in his behavior. Tillie had become her brother's self-appointed personal policeman, and Willie was fed up with her hovering and policing. It was at that moment (of being completely fed-up!) that Willie finally made up his mind. Never again would he copy any more books to write his research reports just to please his sister and be done with the assignment. Besides, he knew it didn't do him any good. He didn't think about one word of what he was writing down. He rushed through it as fast as he could so Tillie would stop nagging him. This time there would be no turning anything in on time, there would be no plagiarized research report on the latest hero, Daniel Boone. In fact, Willie didn't care if he never turned in another report ever again. He would take the failing grade for the report as well as the failing grade in history, whether his sister Tillie liked it or not. Willie had simply decided that he, heroes and history would part ways.

Of course, he didn't tell his sister any of this. He knew that she would never understand. Tillie would never ever be satisfied to give up and fail history. Failure of any kind was her worst fear. She enjoyed getting A's on her research reports and often finished them long before they were due. Tillie Venturely was very proud of the fact that she always got the top grade in the class on her research reports. She easily mastered the note card organizing system, and couldn't understand why Willie couldn't keep his cards together.

Tillie instantly spotted the compass on Willie's lap. "And what's that thing?" she asked, while snatching the compass.

Willie tried to prevent her, but it was too late. Tillie was quick and had already taken a fast step back from him. She eagerly examined the compass and suddenly burst out (as if she were Columbus discovering America), "Look! I bet you didn't see this! There's some writing on the back of it: 'S.S. Ship Shop, Admiral Wright.' You had better return it, or else I will." Tillie thought for a moment and said, "Better yet, let's both return it."

But Willie wasn't listening. He was trying to remember where he had heard of the S.S. Ship Shop and Admiral Wright. Then he remembered a nautical store he had passed a few days earlier, but the doors had been locked. So he had pressed his nose against the windows and peered in. He had seen long rows of glass cases filled with many odd-shaped objects: tomahawks, bows and arrows, a pipe with feathers, bronze canisters, green binoculars of all different sizes and a brass horn, which he wanted to give a good blast on. Willie had been thrilled to see the variety of strange objects, and he couldn't wait to go into the shop and explore. When Willie turned to leave, he had seen a funny looking sign made out of a ship's wheel above the shop's red door. Written around the wheel were the following words:

Admiral Wright's Ship Shop Curios and Collectibles Where only the Curious Dare to Venture.

Before Willie could remember any more, he winced. He felt pain from a pinch on his arm. He knew it came from Tillie. Willie looked up and saw her ready to give him another blast with long-winded words. Tillie stood between him and the door, so there was no opportunity for him to escape the "I know what is good for you" lecture. Willie put his head down and tried to ignore her by starting to fish again in his desk. It didn't work, because Tillie pulled on his earlobe and spoke her words directly into his ear. "You didn't hear anything I just said, did you?" "What were you daydreaming about this time? You never listen to anybody who knows what's good for you and you never pay attention in class. Why are you so interested in desk fishing anyway? What I said, if you had been listening, was that I'm going to call home to let our nanny, Miss Chatterberry, the one you don't listen to either, know that we won't be back from school on time, because we're returning something you found."

Willie continued to keep his head down while he fished, he didn't want to look up until Tillie's blast was over.

"You've been like this ever since we left London!" Tillie continued, as she started to pick up her coat. "Plus, you never get home on time, you never do your homework and you turn in your research reports late. This is all because you spend too much time chasing around on your bike after junk you call collectibles!"

"Can I just have my compass back?" asked Willie as he grabbed the compass from Tillie's hand. He was fast like his sister, and before she had a chance to stop him, he had pushed past her and dashed to the door. He had had enough of her shrill speeches for now. He was used to her lectures, but this one was longer and more unbearable than usual. Tillie scowled after him. She was completely fed up with her embarrassing brother coming late to class, not paying attention to the history lessons, and mostly for ignoring her when she spoke.

"I was about to give it back," said Tillie, as Willie hurried out the door. "Besides, what's so great about that funny looking compass anyway?"

But her brother didn't hear those last words because he was already heading down the road. Tillie watched her brother leave and yelled after him, "You forgot your raincoat again!"

Willie didn't hear, because he was busy fingering the compass and thinking about the magnificent Shiny Shiny Silver Ship, the helpless parrot, the spinning compass and the Ship Shop where only the curious dared to venture.

Chapter Two

The Ship Shop Encounter

Willie really didn't mind that his sister wanted to return the compass, because he wanted to go to the Ship Shop and meet the unknown Admiral Wright. Tillie ran to catch up with her brother, whose clothes were already half-soaked from the rain. Willie didn't notice. He was too excited about going to the Ship Shop. He believed with his whole heart that something mysterious and adventurous was up ahead.

Tillie sped past her brother, waving her arms while shouting, "I passed you!" Willie couldn't stand Tillie's boasting, so he powered his legs, imagining them to be rockets, and zoomed past her.

Tillie snickered, "You're such a show-off." Her words were interrupted by a loud thunderclap.

Willie slowed to a stop and gazed up at the sky, looking for any sign of what he had seen earlier. He immediately saw the Shiny Shiny Silver Ship. It was fighting its way through black clouds and strong winds.

"There it is!" Willie gasped.

"There's what?" yelled Tillie, as she caught up with him. She stopped to brush a strand of hair from her eyes.

"It's the ship I saw this afternoon," Willie said, pointing up to the sky. He began to jump up and down, hardly able to contain his enthusiasm.

Tillie stared into the clouds. "You're daydreaming again, I don't see a thing!" Indeed, she didn't see a thing, because the ship had slipped behind a black cloud.

Willie turned to Tillie and looked her straight in the eyes. He again pointed to the sky and with a firm voice said, "There is a flying silver ship up there fighting its way through those clouds and it looks like Captain Hook's pirate ship from *Peter Pan*."

Tillie rolled her eyes and shook her head, not believing one word her brother said. She began to mock Willie by flapping her arms and saying, "I'm Wendy and I can fly!" With the last word, 'fly' barely out of her mouth, Tillie suddenly shot up and flew into the air, shrieking with the shrillest voice imaginable, "GET ME DOWN RIGHT NOW!" A ship's anchor had dropped from the sky and snagged her backpack, lifting her high into the clouds!

"I would say that was remarkably good

timing. What do you think, Captain? It seems poor Willie, young chap, has had enough of dear sister Tillie for one day. I daresay we should bring her directly to the Ship Shop, and do it quickly." The one who spoke was a portly but very distinguished British Admiral, who was leaning over the ship's rail and peering through binoculars.

"Aye, there's a good idea, Admiral Wright," said the green parrot perched on his shoulder. "But what about Willie?" The Admiral held an open umbrella, so the parrot was safe from the rain. He pulled out a cracker and began to eat it. The ship began to descend.

"He'll get to the Ship Shop fast enough, I suspect, but it is very likely that he may need a bit of my assistance," said the Admiral, with a gentleman's chuckle.

Willie ran as fast as he could to keep up with Tillie, who continued to make it quite clear that she was very unhappy dangling from the ship's anchor.

"Get me off this thing and how many times do I need to say it!" Tillie screeched.

Willie hadn't remembered his sister being that angry since the time he put a large green toad in her backpack as an April Fool's Day joke. He looked up at the anchor where Tillie was still dangling. Willie wasn't too worried for his sister's safety, because the anchor looked very strong, and she was attached securely. Willie shouted up to Tillie, secretly wishing that he were the one flying,

"Don't worry, I think you're headed to the Ship Shop!"

A booming and very British voice broke through the cloud from the deck of the Shiny Shiny Silver Ship. "That's right, Merriweather Mates! We are off to the Ship Shop on Spinnaker Way! Tillie, now, don't you fret, you should be finding the view quite spectacular from up there! And you, Willie, meet us on the rooftop and speed the feet!"

"Now I think I shall apply just a modicum of my assistance to the situation," chuckled the Admiral.

A strange gust of wind blew around Willie and took his feet on a very fast flight. He was flying and cartwheeling through the air. Before he knew it, he was on the doorstep of the nautical store, feeling breathless, having taken the wildest ride of his life.

"Wow, that was fun!" said Willie, as he looked up to see Tillie and the ship, circling above the rooftop.

Willie noticed that the Ship Shop's red door was wide open. Once again, Willie saw the ship wheel sign and his eyes caught the words, *'Where only the Curious Dare to Venture.'* Willie was feeling curious and he was daring to venture, so he excitedly entered the dimly lit shop. Tingles prickled his skin. Something new and different was about to happen and he was not scared, not in the slightest! Willie was a true adventurer, one of those who looked for challenges and welcomed them as opportunities for discovery and change. Willie liked learning new things, but at school he didn't like learning because he couldn't stand those boring encyclopedic readings from Miss Dullywinkle (though she meant well). Nor did he like sitting in one place like at a cramped school desk for a long time, because it made his legs stiff and his bottom sore. When that occurred, Willie was not ready to learn anything, especially history.

In the dimly lit shop, Willie searched for a stairwell. He knew there had to be stairs somewhere. Willie's eyes scanned the room until he found a winding stairway hidden in the back corner next to a long row of bookcases. The winding stairway had stairs that were very small and close together. Willie thought they looked like they belonged in a submarine. He began to climb the too narrow stairs and decided to count each one, even though taking the extra time seemed like the wrong thing to do, especially when his twin sister was dangling from an anchor. But Willie went ahead and excitedly counted each stair as he made his way up. He couldn't wait to tell Tillie exactly how many he had climbed to reach the top. When Willie arrived on that very last stair, he shouted one hundred twenty-three, although no one was around to hear or be impressed!

Willie faced a yellow rooftop door with small black letters on it, which read, *This Door Opens To The Rooftop*. Willie opened the door and a gentle breeze greeted him. The rain had stopped and the sky was clearing. He had no trouble spotting Tillie. She and the Shiny Shiny Silver Ship were above him, and they were at least fifty feet in the air. Tillie wasn't screaming anymore, but she was pumping her legs furiously in the air, trying to pull free.

The Shiny Shiny Silver Ship circled overhead

with Tillie swinging back and forth like the pendulum of a crazy clock.

Tillie started to screech again, "Pleeeeeze, somebody up there get me off this thing!"

Willie noted Tillie's unusual 'pleeeeeze.' He figured his sister had become a bit nicer because she could not fix her predicament by her own wits and efforts. Tillie would have to rely on someone else to help her and this was something that she did not like!

The Admiral leaned over the ship's rail and spoke loudly. "Tillie, hold on, dear mate, I suspect you shall be down soon! Ho there, Willie! Mind the cleat! With a bit of your help I will bring her in!"

Willie yelled back, "Aye aye!" but he wasn't sure who the Admiral would bring in, the flying ship, or Tillie, or both. He also wasn't sure what a cleat was, but being the kind of boy that he was, curious and clever, he thought it might be the big metal object on the end of the rooftop. He ran across the roof to the funny looking two-pronged metal thing and looked up, trying to figure out what to do.

Willie thought about what he could do and then he saw the Admiral skillfully glide the ship towards him so that Tillie could stretch out her hand, just inches above his head.

"Grab my hands!" Willie shouted, as he reached up towards his sister.

Tillie tried to grab on, but she slipped out of her brother's grip and jerked upwards. Willie yelled again, "Don't worry, I'll rescue you!"

A coil of silver rope suddenly dropped from the Shiny Shiny Silver Ship, and Willie caught it easily and made a lasso (in only a matter of seconds). With the speed and precision of a rodeo star, he circled the rope above his head, lassoed the anchor and then tied the other end of the rope to the cleat. Willie's incredible display of skill and expertise surprised himself and his sister too! Perhaps he was even more surprised when the ship jerked to a halt and quickly lowered its anchor and allowed Tillie's feet to touch the rooftop. And of course, once Tillie's feet touched the rooftop, she eagerly wiggled out of her backpack. It was interesting to note that the rope was no longer holding taut to the anchor because Willie's (not so carefully tied) knot had slipped out. Now one might think (and rightly so!) that the ship would no longer be steadied. However, quite miraculously and for reasons unknown, the Shiny Shiny Silver Ship remained steadfastly suspended so much so that the slightest movement could not be detected.

Willie ran over to Tillie, who was trying to wipe the scuff marks off her shoes. She hadn't suffered one bruise for such an adventurous ride, but now that it was over, it was the black marks on her white shoes she was most concerned with.

"Don't worry about the scuff marks, just look at that ship!" said Willie while gazing at the ship.

"They're not on your shoes," said Tillie, as she struggled to wipe off the marks.

Tillie finally gave up and joined Willie in staring at the mysteriously suspended Shiny Shiny Silver Ship. The twins were amazed to behold its perfect stillness, anchored as it was by absolutely nothing. The stillness was broken by the quick drop of a very purple rope ladder and the appearance of a very distinguished gentlemanly figure wearing an admiral's uniform. He had a green parrot perched on his shoulder. The interesting pair began a brisk descent down the ladder.

"It's the Admiral!" shouted Willie.

"Of course it's an Admiral," said Tillie, beginning to recover from her dangle.

The Admiral announced in a big booming

voice, "Well done, mates, simply outstanding! I could not have done better myself!" The interesting twosome continued their descent down the rope ladder. An open umbrella suddenly appeared and the Admiral held it over his head with one hand as he carried a steamer trunk in the other. The parrot whistled a little tune, and to the careful listening ear it was *Yankee Doodle Dandy*, but to other ears (inattentive ones) it was just noise. The colorful pair amazed and delighted Willie. Tillie did not want to be amazed or delighted.

The distinguished Admiral wore a navy blue admiral's coat, with bright brass buttons, stiffly pressed trousers and on his head was an admiral's hat. The parrot also wore a navy blue admiral's coat and an admiral's hat, which tipped to one side, because it was a bit big for his head.

The Admiral carried an umbrella that had a swirling rainbow pattern that never seemed to be the same, because it swirled as he moved, and when it caught the light, it gleamed and shimmered like the sail of the ship. When the pair arrived at the bottom rung of the very purple rope ladder, the Admiral chuckled and bowed, and made a grand sweeping motion with his arm as he put the trunk down.

"Mates, I see you both are well and without a scratch to show for such thrills," the Admiral said. "The Captain and I are truly delighted, overjoyed, enraptured, enchanted and most definitely honored to be in your presence."

Before Willie and Tillie could blink an eye, they saw the trunk fly through the air and land exactly next to them. Before they could blink again, they saw the Admiral (with the Captain still perched on his shoulder) jump off the very purple rope ladder with a very bouncy bounce. The trunk landed without a dent and the umbrella landed without one slight bent. The Admiral also landed sturdily on one knee and then somersaulted like a speeding ball to the feet of Willie and Tillie. Somehow (and only the Admiral knows how) Captain Perry Parrot managed to stay on the Admiral's shoulder despite the speedy rolling.

The Admiral reached into his coat pocket and pulled out a round metal object and sat down on the trunk next to Willie and Tillie. With one leg crossed over the other, the Admiral paused, to study the object.

The Admiral took a very long breath (for dramatic effect, of course!) and most proudly declared, "Excellent, indeed! According to the geographical and temporal readings of my Quantum Space Atomic Clock, which precisely counts the vibrations of atoms to measure the passing of time, I declare that my calculations for our arrival are exactly perfect!"

With that last word, the generously pro-portioned Admiral stood up, put the Quantum Space Atomic Clock back in his coat pocket, took off his white gloves and began to brush the dust off his trousers. He then reached over to pick up the umbrella (still open) and bowed as if he were a conductor about to lead an orchestra.

Willie and Tillie could not say anything. They were astonished at the amazing and somewhat strange entrance of such interesting characters. Willie immediately noticed that the Admiral's eyes were as blue as the bluest ocean, and fantastically alive and bright. He had bushy eyebrows and an even bushier mustache that looked like the bottom of a broom.

The Captain's face was perky and alert. His beak was round, and somewhat large for a parrot. Without a doubt, the most distinguishing and most unusual feature of the Captain was a long red beard, which grew directly under his beak, and would trouble him when it came to his cracker eating habits. (This we shall observe later!)

As Willie and Tillie continued to watch the Admiral and the Captain, they both felt that the unusual pair were characters that they had known sometime before and had been familiar friends with, even though this was the first time they had ever met.

Chapter Three

Meet the Admiral and the Captain

The Admiral leaned down to Willie and Tillie and said, "Forgive me for not introducing myself and my loyal Captain and first mate. Do let me begin." And so he did: "Merriweather Mates, I am Admiral Wright, an historical adventurer and truth seeker, who studies the words and deeds of heroes, indomitable individuals who were mighty and powerful in thoughts, words and actions. There were no empty promises and false boasts with these truest of characters. They simply said what they meant and did what they said, a rare phenomenon indeed!

"Speaking of truest of characters"—the Admiral suddenly motioned to the parrot, still perched on his shoulder— "I am very pleased to introduce Captain Perry Parrot, a brave and true character, who has proven himself to be a most faithful companion and friend. He has been by my side through all our adventures, never abandoned ship when the seas were stormy, and I predict that he will never forsake me on my voyages to come."

The Captain settled back on the Admiral's shoulder, and pulled a cracker out of his beard.

The Admiral continued, "Together we journey in our glorious, grandiose, greatly beloved, Shiny Shiny Silver Ship with its magnificent silvery shine, which you have undoubtedly noticed. We voyage in this fantastic and mysterious flying vessel to places where we are stunned, awed and dazzled. Our sole purpose is to search the world, the universe, and the outer galactic regions, if necessary, to discover history's finest, and truest of characters, heroes of the highest kind, Character Champions! Indeed a very worthy name for champions of outstanding character!"

While the Admiral continued his speech, Captain Perry began to munch on the cracker, as one would snack on popcorn during a very long movie.

"Character Champions lead lives of faith, wisdom, courage and valor. Such character is worth emulating, for these champions have inspired countless generations to better service and sacrifice for others."

It was a long speech, and Willie couldn't quite figure out all of what the Admiral meant by it, but he was interested to find out about something new. The Admiral's enthusiasm made Willie want to learn whatever emulating, faith, wisdom, valor, sacrifice and service might mean.

Tillie liked the Admiral's speech, too, because she knew almost all of the big words he had used, including the word "emulating," which means to become just like something. (To emulate a heroic character means to act like a hero, someone who is courageous, wise, honest and good.) Tillie liked history and historical characters, and she felt she knew many of them already. The Admiral's speech warmed Tillie's heart, so she no longer wanted to hold a grudge against him or the Captain for snagging her backpack with the ship's anchor.

The Admiral closed his swirling rainbow umbrella and put it under one arm and picked up the trunk and said, "Shall the Merriweather Mates scurry their feet, along with ours, to the

Ship Shop's Heroical Storical Laboratory?"

"What's that?" asked Willie and Tillie together, while feeling somewhat baffled.

"Good question, mates! I was about to tell you," said the Admiral, clearing his throat as if he were trying to clear his thoughts. "The Heroical Storical Laboratory is simply the outrageously wonderful secret laboratory located deep under my spectacular Ship Shop. In the Heroical Storical Laboratory, extremely intriguing stories known as Heroical Storicals are told about the outstanding heroic characters. Now, these stories are not figments of my imagination or anyone else's, but they are exciting truth-filled adventures from history. Heroical Storicals are all about heroes, champions of good character, whose faith, courage, words and deeds earn them a rightful place in my very distinguished gallery, the one and only, never been duplicated, Admiral Wright's Heroes' Great Wall of Faith.

"I might add, mates, that these extremely intriguing stories are gathered from many excellent and trustworthy sources, like the hero's personal letters, diaries, journals and collectibles. Such important items reveal the heart of the Character Champion: their passion and their commitments, and of course (the Admiral's voice began to get softer) such discovery leads to fantastic treasure."

"You mean like gold?" Willie asked eagerly, but right away, he felt slightly embarrassed and wished he hadn't said it. He didn't want the Admiral to think of him as being greedy.

"No, not gold," said the Admiral, as he gave Willie a small pat on the head. "These treasures are more valuable than gold because one is led to truth, knowledge and understanding."

"About what?" asked Tillie, who was feeling pleased that she asked the question before her brother did.

With a sudden dramatic sweep of his arm,

the Admiral lifted his umbrella and aimed it to the sky and said, "Heroes of the Highest Kind, those incomparable and invincible champions of outstanding character, Character Champions, whose words and deeds have inspired countless generations to better service..."

"...and sacrifice for others," interrupted Captain Perry Parrot, who was just finishing his cracker and was starting to yawn. Willie and Tillie noticed more cracker crumbs falling from his open beak, and the Captain noticed them watching him. He looked sheepish and began to brush the crumbs off the Admiral's shoulder, who pretended not to notice.

"Eh, thank you, Captain. I must admit I do get carried away at times with my speeches. I am sorry, I am just a bit impassioned about heroes, those indomitable Character Champions," said the Admiral, as he brought his umbrella back down from its point and continued to speak. "On my travels with the Captain, I have found collectibles from the lives and times of the heroes. They are clues into the truth about who the Character Champions really were." The Admiral's voice began to get lower and quieter. "These mysteries I will reveal from the bottom of my trunk." He lowered his voice to a whisper as he spoke the last few words and said nothing for a few moments.

Willie was concerned and wondered whether the Admiral was feeling well. "What's wrong?" he asked.

The Admiral burst out with a booming voice. "Nothing at all, mates! I wanted to see if your ears were listening, wax can build up, you know! Allow me to lead the way down to my Heroical Storical Laboratory beneath my marvelous spiral stairway—which, by the way, has one hundred twenty three stairs that Willie has already correctly counted and failed to mention to his beloved sister."

Willie wondered how he knew he had counted the stairs.

The Admiral continued to Willie, "You have a definite mind for details, and the making of a true Heroical-Storical-Observicorical-Researchorical-Scientifical-Mate." He said this last part in one quick breath.

"What's that?" Willie and Tillie asked together, and turned to look at each other in surprise.

"What the Admiral means, more simply put," said the Captain, still brushing cracker crumbs off the Admiral's shoulder, "is that a Heroical-Storical-Observicorical-Researchorical-Scientifical-Mate is a character who likes to figure things out. Heroical-Storical-Observicorical-Researchorical-Scientifical-Mates ask questions to find reasonable answers, and, of course they're willing to try their best, because they care about others and themselves. They also happen to be very curious about heroes who are champions of good character. That's the heroical part. The storical part has to do with an extremely intriguing story about the hero's outstanding deeds of courage and sacrifice. The observicorical part has to do with paying attention to the hero's storical, asking inquisitive questions and not missing one detail because of a somewhat serious problem called Mind Wander. This happens when a mind floats around from this to that and does not focus on what it is hearing and thinking about."

"A very real Heroical-Storical-Observicorical-Researchorical-Scientifical-Mate does not engage in much Mind Wander," interrupted the Admiral as he put his finger to his forehead and continued. "Mind Wander is a most unaware place to be in. Mates, like you, must discipline their thoughts to pay attention to knowledge, which is mostly gained from study and experience, so that the mind may learn and grow. Very important indeed! Continue on, Captain, you are doing outstandingly well with your explanation."

The Captain began again, with a bit more puff in his chest. "Thanks, Admiral, for the compliment. Encouragement and affirmation do wonders for my confidence."

The Captain continued, "The researchorical part has to do with a close and careful examination of a hero's storical, or any other subject or problem. The scientifical part has to do with a careful and orderly approach to the study of a hero's storical or anything else." The Captain paused and took a cloth out to wipe his brow. "Whew, that is quite enough explaining about that very, very long word."

"I agree," said Willie. "Besides, I don't know if I can remember all of what that very, very long word means!"

"Well, I can remember!" said Tillie with a

flip of her ponytail.

"Remember what you can, but don't forget that the more you think and act like a Heroical-Storical-Observicorical-Researchorical-Scientifical Mate, the more you will remember what the very, very long word means," said the Admiral.

"Is the mate in that very, very long word a Character Champion too?" asked Willie.

"Yes, indeedy!" shouted the Admiral, while slapping his knee. "A Character Champion is a very solid thinking character, besides being a very solid acting character! A solid thinking and acting character is a Heroical-Storical-Observicorical-Researchorical-Scientifical Mate simply because they practice the skills of reasonable clear thinking and acting right!"

"I think I understand what you mean," said Willie. "Your thoughts and actions should not be confused if you are a real Character Champion, because you need a clear head to think and do what is right, especially when you are helping and caring about others."

"Well, I completely understand the Admiral's point and I don't need to say it!" said Tillie with a flip of her ponytail.

"Might I add another very important point about Character Champions?" asked the Captain.

"What's that?" asked Willie.

"Character Champions are also heroes with Faith Power!" shouted the Captain, as he took off his hat and threw it high into the air. The Captain's hat landed back on his head exactly crooked the way it was before.

"Faith Power? I have never heard of that! But what I want to know is, how did you do that with your hat?" asked Willie.

"How I did that with my hat is a secret! But Faith Power will not be a secret! Yes indeed, you must know about such a phenomena!" said the Captain.

"Phenomawhat?" asked Willie.

"That means anything which is extremely unusual, and Faith Power is quite unusual and wonderful. Faith Power enables one to step out into the unknown and believe the impossible when the improbable is all around." The Admiral turned to the Captain. "Please explain how the Heroical-Storical-Observicorical-Researchorical-Scientifical-Mates, in search of good and reasonable answers, study collectibles, diaries, journals, letters, maps and even trunks or anything else that would help them on their quest for truth and understanding."

The Admiral now stood directly in front of the Captain, who was looking down at his long red beard, as he combed it, trying very hard to get all the cracker crumbs out of it.

The Captain looked up and put his small comb back into his pocket and said. "Very well Admiral, now that the crumbs are gone,

I shall carry on with explaining." The Captain straightened up, and raised his wing tip and began his speech, as if he was a professor in front of a large class of students. "Indeed, a Heroical-Storical-Observicorical-Researchorical-Scientifical-Mate studies and examines collectibles acquired from the hero's life, and such collectibles could be anything from a boot to a book, a hairbrush to a hat, or a curler to a comb. The goal in such study and examination is to gain correct ideas and understand the true truth about the hero's life and definitely not the wrong truth. True truth, as I have learned from the Admiral, is always based on a reasonable estimation and deduction of the facts. Of course, the facts must always be gathered from the best and most reliable sources. If you wanted to know about the world of rocket science, for instance, you would read a book on the subject or talk to someone who works as a rocket scientist. Most certainly, you wouldn't find much help from a character who was a botanist, one who studies plants, (unless of course, the botanist studied and built rockets in his free time). Sherlock Holmes, the great fictional detective, created by the very imaginative Sir Arthur Conan Doyle, did the same sort of thing. Holmes and his dear friend, Doctor Watson, used clear reasoning once they gathered information from the best possible sources, then they simply used their eyes, ears, noses and instincts to help them find out if something was true or not or if someone was telling the truth or not."

"Oh," said Willie, "I think I get it, a heroical researchorical...uh, mate is like a detective searching for truth and knowledge about history, heroes or anything else he or she is curious about. I remember a time when I found a bird's nest and I wanted to know what kind of bird laid the egg and what tree it fell out of so I could return the nest to its mom. I looked for clues around the schoolyard trees to see if there were any broken eggshells around, to tell me I might be close to the tree where the nest fell."

"Precisely," pronounced the Admiral with a bright smile. (He only said this when he felt that his ideas were being understood.) "I might add that you, Willie, are on the way to becoming a true Heroical-Storical-Observicorical-Researchorical-Scientifical-Mate, even if you cannot say it quite properly yet." He gave Willie a wink.

"What about me?" asked Tillie.

The Admiral quickly added, "Of course, of course. You, dear mate, are on your way too. You are also fearless in asking questions."

The Admiral reached into his coat pocket and produced a red lab coat which he quickly unfolded. It had large white letters printed on the back, reading Heroical-Storical-Observicorical-Researchorical-Scientifical-Mate. In very small white letters underneath, it read "Under Construction." He handed the coat to Tillie.

"I want one too," said Willie.

"Well, I have one for you too, and it's blue, like the color of my coat," said the Admiral as he peeled Willie's blue coat from the front of Tillie's red one. "Now, mates, with no further ado, let us descend into the depths of my Heroical Storical Laboratory!"

Willie and Tillie put their lab coats on as the Admiral turned and headed to the rooftop door.

"Can you teach me, Admiral," said Willie, "to say that very, very long word?"

The Admiral turned around and was just about to answer when the Captain suddenly blurted out, "Stop, right there! You forgot to give the mates some extremely important certain things that go into the upper right pockets of their lab coats."

"I did? Why, what things are you referring

to?" asked the Admiral as he quickly turned to the Captain. "Of course, oh my! How could I forget?" he explained while throwing his hands up to express his mild upset. "The mates are missing ink pens and miniature sized clipboards with note observation pads! Heroical-Storical-Observicorical-Researchorical-Scientifical-Mates must always have these important tools in good working order." He paused for a moment and stroked his mustache. "Pens and clipboards can be used to jot down your observations, gained from seeing and hearing that which is going on around you. Observation jotting will help you remember what you learn so that you can grow in understanding, and I might add, mates, that when this is happening you are embarking on a very exciting adventure of discovery."

The Admiral brought out the ink pens, miniature clipboards and note observation pads, so that Willie and Tillie could be perfectly outfitted in the most official uniform of a Heroical-Storical-Observicorical-Researchorical-Scientifical-Mate. The Admiral placed the pens and clipboards in the upper right pocket of their lab coats.

The Admiral paused and took a step back to study Willie and Tillie. He scratched his head and said. "Umm, something is still missing and it may be more than one thing."

"I know exactly what's missing," said the Captain. "It's pocket protectors! Pocket protectors serve the purpose of preventing unsightly ink marks on fresh new lab coat pockets."

"Of course, of course," said the Admiral. "A pocket protector is one of the things that is missing." He quickly pulled out two very yellow plastic pocket protectors and handed them to Willie and Tillie. "There you are!" The twins excitedly inserted the yellow plastic protectors into their coat pockets. They carefully placed their ink pens and miniature clipboards inside their protectors. Willie and Tillie wondered how they looked now that they were completely and officially Observicorical-Researchorical Mates.

"You both look very serious and scientific indeed, well on your way to becoming Heroical-Storical-Observicorical-Researchorical-Scientifical-Mates," said the Admiral. "But, let me warn you: You must practice the skills of being a heroical-Storical-Observicorical-Researchorical-Scientifical-Mate in order to become one. Wearing the outfit is not enough; you must act like one. You do not become a talented musician by sitting on the piano bench. You must put your fingers on the keys and practice the notes. Image is not necessarily reality. You must practice and practice to become Heroical-Storical-Observicorical-Researchorical-Scientifical-Mates by doing over and over what real Heroical-Storical-Observicorical-Researchorical-Scientifical-Mates do. They ask questions and they think, perhaps another rare phenomenon." The Admiral stopped and said "hmmmm" to himself. Then he took a deep loud breath. "They try to come up with reasonable reasons for what they know and understand and such mates know enough to have the courage to know that they don't know everything." The Admiral made a funny face by scrunching his nose and wrinkling his brow. "My goodness, that's far too many knows!

"Anyhoo, enough of such discussion, it likely makes little sense to you now, but soon you will understand more of what I mean as we learn and grow. Nevertheless, I have provided you with all the necessary and proper tools to help you focus, observe, and avoid the dreadful state of Mind Wander. Finally, there is one extra-special-out-of-the-ordinary-most-important-something you do not have yet." You need the Extraordinary Black-Rimmed Glasses, which mysteriously appeared in the

Admiral's hand.

Tillie's jaw dropped open. "I'm not wearing those!" she said. "They're ugly."

"I like them, and I will wear them," said Willie.

"Wearing them will come later," said the Admiral. "Such Extraordinary Black-Rimmed Glasses have a very special purpose that will be appreciated at another time—you will be most surprised."

The Admiral delicately placed the glasses in Willie and Tillie's very yellow plastic pocket protectors as if the glasses had some sort of special powers.

The Admiral took a step back and admired Willie and Tillie. "I can now declare you to be wearing the complete and true official uniform of a Heroical-Storical-Observicorical-Researchorical-Scientifical-Mate, and, might I add that you both look absolutely, perfectly, wonderfully greeeat!

With no more unnecessary delays, then, shall we proceed down the stairs?" He turned and began to walk toward the rooftop door.

Over his shoulder he said, "By the way, this will be a perfect opportunity to learn how to say this most terribly difficult word." The Admiral stopped to think for a minute and, twisting his mustache, said, "I say, perhaps if we break it up into small sounds and put it to a tune, it will become very easy to learn. Try this: 'HE-ROW-E-CULL-STORE-E-CULL-OB-SER-VE-COR-E-CULL-RE-SER-CHOR-E-CULL-SI-EN-TI-FI-CULL-MATE! Repeat after me, along with the beat of our feet as we step down my marvelous stairway, all the wonders of which, by the way, you have not yet seen."

The Captain fluttered down from the Admiral's shoulder and followed him toward the rooftop door and the marvelous stairway, with Tillie and Willie close behind.

"What's he talking about? He is a bit on

the nutty side, don't you think?" whispered Tillie to Captain Perry, who now flew close by her side.

"Nutty? Nutty?" whispered the Captain to Tillie. "Certainly not, trust me, the Admiral knows exactly what he is saying and why he is saying it. He has a brilliant mind indeed! I have been around him quite some time, so I should know more than anyone. What the Admiral means is that his marvelous stairway has more going on than you think!"

"Like what?" asked Willie, who overheard the conversation. "I want to see something now!"

"Patience! Wait and see," said the Captain. "'Don't hurry a moment,' the Admiral always says. 'Moments happen soon enough, and they always manage to arrive at the right time and never the wrong time.'"

"Mates," said the Admiral, who was already heading down the winding staircase, "do I hear useless chatter? Get ready to clear your throats to sing. My throat is clear and I am beginning this moment. If you listen to the beat of your feet on the stairs, I suspect you shall find your tune! All you have to do is try!"

"I'm not good at singing," said Tillie, "and I don't want to."

Willie didn't mind trying to sing, especially since he was starting to have that same feeling that something surprising and wonderful was up ahead.

The Admiral's scratchy but amazing, in-tune voice boomed in perfect synchronization with his steps on the stairs. Before Willie and Tillie could fully realize what was happening, they, too, were singing, but only because they found the courage to try the first note. Together with Captain Perry, they were soon singing the marvelous Heroical-Storical-Observicorical-Researchorical-Scientifical-Mate song, but they were assisted by something strange that was happening on the marvelous stairway. With each step that Willie and Tillie took on the winding stairway, the beat of their feet released the sounds of a bongo band. This, of course, added much power and rhythm to their voices. They heard sounds of all kinds of Latin percussion instruments, like bongos, congas and timbales. They also heard flutes, clarinets and an entire brass section! (Imagine that!) Such magnificent musical support gave Willie and Tillie the confidence they needed to say as well as sing the Heroical-Storical-Observicorical-Researchorical-Scientifical-Mate song. It was also helpful that the Admiral and Captain sang so enthusiastically. It was quite a scene to observe: Admiral Wright, Captain Perry Parrot, Willie and Tillie, bouncing and bongoing down a winding stairwell, belting out a song that made very little sense to anyone who did not understand.

Chapter Four

More About the Heroical Storical Laboratory

After the singing, drumming, bouncing, bongoing group arrived at the bottom of the winding stairs, the Admiral announced, "Willie and Tillie, you officially deserve the title 'Merriweather Mates' because I can see you are very merry, indeed!"

The group faced a dark blue door trimmed with gold paint that sparkled in the light. On it was written in white lettering: "Heroical-Storical-Laboratory"and written in fine print below were the words: "Everyone Out But The

Curious." The Admiral began to sing a silly ditty as he reached into his coat pocket to find the right key to open the door. The ditty went something like this:

"Oh ye Merriweather Mates
Better to make merry
Than to be dreary
Because merry doeth the heart good
And dreary ah not so good."

Tillie was laughing, and, of course, Willie was too. Willie tried to stop laughing, but he discovered that in trying to stop, he laughed more, so he kept trying to stop, because he wanted to keep laughing more.

"Now, mates, what I hear is that you are having too much fun! Now, that is good indeed!" said the Admiral, while he fumbled for his keys, making jangling noises as he looked in his coat pocket. "Oh, bother, where is that key? The mysteries of my Heroical Storical Laboratory await us and the key is nowhere to be found! Dash!"

Finally, the Admiral pulled out a large gold key ring with exactly one hundred brightly colored petite keys that were a very shiny red, yellow or blue.

Willie's eyes opened wide. "I've never seen that many keys! What do they all open?" asked Willie as he reached to touch them.

"They open many doors, cupboards and trunks," said the Admiral. "Remember that even though something is a bit small and petite it can still do the job." The Admiral straightened his jacket and plucked off a tiny piece of white lint.

"How do you know which key opens which door, cupboard or trunk?" asked Tillie.

"Why, it can be a challenge," said the Admiral, "but it can also be simple if you, ah, follow your..." The Admiral stopped talking and stretched his arm to lift off the Captain's hat.

The Captain squawked. "What are you doing?"

"Aah, here is that key," said the Admiral. "My hunch was correct; it was tucked away in the Captain's hat. As I was going to say, keys can be found in the strangest of places." The Admiral peeled away an inside flap from the Captain's hat and brought out a very small silver key, this one about the size of a paper clip.

"How did you figure out where the key was?" asked Tillie.

"You had to know it was there all the time," said Willie.

"Not necessarily," said the Admiral. "I have learned many times over the years that things, especially keys, can turn up in the most oddest of places, so I naturally check the odd places first."

"Good idea," said Willie. "I'll try that next time."

"Can I have my hat back, please?" asked the Captain, who was quickly smoothing his ruffled head feathers. He never liked having his feathers ruffled. The Captain thought himself a proper and orderly bird, even though he could be a bit clumsy from time to time.

"My apologies, Captain," said the Admiral, as he tossed the hat into the air.

Captain Perry Parrot fluttered up into the air to catch his hat, and of course, it landed perfectly crooked on his head just like before.

"Mates, the Heroical Storical Laboratory awaits us, and there is much to tell, see and do," said the Admiral, as he opened the door with the petite shiny silver key.

The group entered a small circular room, which was paneled in oak wood. On its circular walls were framed pictures of heroic characters and above each of the pictures was a bronze plaque with the words "Honorary and Distinguished Member of Admiral Wright's

Heroes' Great Wall of Faith."

"Are these your family?" asked Tillie while walking up to examine the pictures more closely.

"Well, not exactly," said the Admiral, "but they are of kindred spirit."

"What does that mean?" asked Willie.

"What the Admiral means by 'kindred spirit' is that these characters up on the wall value what the Admiral treasures," the Captain answered. He took off his hat and tried to smooth down more of his head feathers.

"Like riches and power?" asked Tillie.

The question jarred the Admiral so that he jumped back, almost knocking the Captain off his shoulder. In the same motion, he opened his colorful swirling umbrella and thrust it upwards. Tillie thought that he looked like a circus ringmaster commanding an audience, as he twirled his umbrella up in the air and then balanced it on a finger. The twirling canopy of the umbrella quickly transformed into a sheet of laser light that beamed red onto all of the portraits of the heroes on the wall.

With a gleam in his eye, the Admiral said, "No, dearest Tillie, riches and power are not what I treasure, nor are they treasured by these outstanding Character Champions."

The Admiral raised his hand high and flashed the red beam back and forth on the heroes' faces as he began to explain why such heroes were worthy of recognition. "Mates, these heroes displayed on my Heroes' Great Wall of Faith are there because they are the truest of true Character Champions, they are courageous, honest, wise and trustworthy. Riches and power are not what Character Champions strive for. They want truth, wisdom, goodness and the effort to do what is right to be foremost in their lives. I might add that the really truest of true Character Champions never insist on taking the first seat of honor, nor do they care if they are thought of as important! Instead, they try to be of service to others, whether or not they expect to receive anything for it. Such helpful and humble deeds are somewhat unusual in the world of characters, but that sort of activity is very ordinary to a real Character Champion. In addition, such Champions can admit when they are wrong, and if another individual has been hurt by their wrongdoing, they can be sorry and really mean it. Take note, mates, for that is a very big thing indeed! Character Champions always try to do their best and never give up when problems come. Finally, mates, the truest of true Character Champions," the Admiral raised his voice quite loud, as if he were giving a last bang on a drum, "have Heroical Storicals that are extremely intriguing and if one comes to understand and appreciate the stories then much opportunity for learning and growing will occur."

At these last few words, the Captain, who had dozed off, woke up and ruffled his feathers.

"That was a very long speech," said Tillie.

"Indeed it was, and I have even a longer one, but that will have to wait for another time, perhaps, or not at all," said the Admiral as he frowned slightly. "I admit, and the Captain does remind me from time to time, that I can say far too many words to explain my ideas. I suppose I shall have to work on that."

"I liked your speech, even though I didn't understand everything," said Willie. "But I think I understand why you have all the hero pictures on your Great Wall of Faith. You want to be reminded of all the heroes from history who were true Character Champions."

"Excellent, mate!" said the Admiral. "You are definitely beginning to grasp the idea of what I am talking about, but, more excellently, you have the attitude of a willing and eager learner."

"I know something," said Tillie, as her eye

caught the Admiral's oversized trunk. "You have lots and lots of Heroical Storicals to tell because your trunk looks like you've got one too..."

"...many collectibles gathered from your travels through history, and lots of them are packed in that old trunk!" shouted Willie, interrupting his sister. Tillie glared at him, not feeling the least bit happy with her brother.

"Excellent deduction, Willie, mate! Sherlock Holmes would have been proud," said the Admiral. "You are thinking and observing like a true Heroical-Storical-Observicorical-Researchorical-Scientifical-Mate.

"I must also say, to you, Tillie, that you made an excellent deduction regarding the fact that I have many, many Heroical Storicals. It is true that the generous size of my steamer trunk is due to an overabundance of collectibles."

The Admiral lowered his hand, and the red

laser light beams became a swirling rainbow umbrella again. He folded up the umbrella and placed it under his arm and said, "Now, a Heroical Storical awaits both of you. By the way, can anyone tell me what a Heroical Storical is?"

"I'll tell you what it is!" shouted Willie, jumping up and down. "A Heroical Storical is simply an extremely intriguing story about an outstanding heroic character from history whose good words and deeds are worth learning from."

"Stupendous, mate, and a nice, concise definition too!" said the Admiral, while slapping his knee with great delight. "For answering the question correctly and practicing the skills of a true Heroical-Storical-Observicorical-Researchorical-Scientifical-Mate, your reward is to wear an Absolutely Genuine Gold Star." The gold star suddenly appeared from under the Admiral's sleeve.

The Admiral lowered his voice and almost whispered, "Mates, note this very important detail on your observation pads. In the year 1848, a certain James Marshall was hired to build a sawmill for a landowner named John Sutter. It was to be located on the American River in the Sacramento Valley in California. One day while he was building the mill, he spotted flecks of yellow in the stream, and those yellow flecks turned out to be none other than absolutely genuine gold! In fact, it was the very same gold that is in this Absolutely Genuine Gold Star! The Captain and I were eyewitnesses to the very historic event of discovering gold. Both John Sutter and James Marshall would have liked to have kept the discovery a secret, but the shop owner who tested the gold to see if it was real was none too quiet about the news. The shop owner spread the news, because he likely wanted more shoppers in his store. A stampede for gold was born and Sutter and Marshall were not happy. Such golden news spread fast, and characters from all over the country and the world arrived with gold fever. Take note, mates; the love of gold is a blind to one's better sight. Such obsession with gold caused many to leave their families and never come home. A good portion of gold seekers never found fame and fortune; instead they came away with rocks of disappointment and feelings of loss, not glittering gold nuggets. Yet, in their disappointment, some likely learned the lesson that all that glitters is not gold, and that abandoning family and friends for the pursuit of it is not wise. Sadly, such golden fevered men failed to recognize that the purest gold is found in pursuing and nurturing the love of those near and dear. Gold nuggets cannot comfort in the day of trouble and dismay, but good friends and family can."

The Admiral straightened up and raised

his voice. "Enough of that story; I am most anxious to have the honor to grant you, Willie, your very first Absolutely Genuine Gold Star."

The Admiral took a bow in honor of Willie and carefully pinned the Absolutely Genuine Gold Star on Willie's lab coat pocket.

"An Absolutely Genuine Gold Star," said Willie while gazing and touching it very carefully. "I am now very special and important!"

"Well, yes, but you have always been special, wonderful and important," the Admiral emphasized. "Because you are You! The only unique You that ever was, is, or will be! An Absolutely Genuine Gold Star doesn't make You a better You! No amount of Absolutely Genuine Gold Stars ever will. Never forget that, mate!"

"Aye, he's right!" said the Captain, as he began to spread some cheese on another cracker. "A You is far more valuable than gold. A You is a living breathing being, made up of all sorts of special wonder, like the wonder of eyes, a nose, a mouth, a heart, a liver, lungs, and kidneys not to mention the wonder of being able to think, laugh, cry, dance, run and leap for joy."

The Admiral continued, "A You is not a hard, cold lump of metal. Even though gold can be hammered, molded, and made into something special, remember that gold will always remain, in its essence, cold and hard. Take note, mates, that those who like gold a bit too much become a bit too cold and hard."

"Can I have an Absolutely Genuine Gold Star, too?" asked Tillie. "I can tell you what a Heroical-Storical-Observicorical-Researchorical-Scientifical-Mate is." Tillie was very pleased with herself for having said the word quickly and perfectly.

"Splendid," said the Admiral. "Tell us, Tillie."

"It's someone who likes Heroical Storicals and they are a very curious character. Such a character wants to learn all they can about everything and they especially want to know all about heroes who are Character Champions. A Heroical-Storical-Observicorical-Researchorical-Scientifical-Mate also asks questions to get to the true truth about the life and times of the hero. And a Heroical-Storical-Observicorical-Researchorical-Scientifical-Mate does what the Captain says, they get answers from a reasonable estimation and deduction of the facts. The facts from heroes' lives are found in trunks, books, letters, journals, maps, collectibles or anything else that is a credible and believable information source."

The Captain quickly stopped eating his cracker, and his head perked up. He was impressed with Tillie's speech, and obviously very pleased to have his name mentioned.

The Admiral was pleasantly astonished that he heard such a speech from Tillie.

"Yes, yes, that's it!" shouted the Captain. "You're getting it! Doesn't she deserve an

Absolutely Genuine Gold Star as well, Admiral?"

"Absolutely," the Admiral answered. "Remember and don't forget mates, that the brilliant minds of Sherlock Holmes and Dr. Watson based answers to questions on the facts they found, from observation and study. They struggled and searched for the best answers to their questions in order to arrive at a reasonable explanation of what happened. Suppose Mr. Holmes stumbled on a large muddy footprint, ten times the size of his shoe. It would not be reasonable for him to guess that the giant muddy footprint came from a small squirrel."

"Or a turtle's foot," added Willie.

"But Mr. Holmes might guess the footprint came from an elephant, because the footprint was big and elephants are very big animals," said Tillie, feeling quite smart.

"Aye, that's the idea," said the Captain.

The thoughts of a Heroical-Storical-Observicorical-Researchorical-Scientifical-Mate are based on facts gained from observation, study, experience and, sometimes, leaps of intuition that lead to good sense, not non-sense."

"Into what?" asked Willie.

"Intuition," said the Admiral. "Behind the word is the idea that a special feeling or sense comes from your..."

"...gut," interrupted the Captain, who thumped his stomach with his wing tip. He continued, "And your gut helps you figure out whether that something is true."

"You mean you think with your stomach?" asked Tillie.

The Captain looked puzzled. "Well, no, not really, it just helps you figure out whether something is true or not. Your gut gives you a sense, or a hunch about something. It's hard to explain—you'll know when it happens."

The Admiral continued, "Now that we have explained some rather important ideas, forgive me, mates, if the Captain and I have bored and perhaps dulled you by being too wordy."

"Oh no, I like hearing what you and the Captain talk about. You're funny and fun!" said Willie.

"For the first time in a long time, I'm learning about things I never knew," said Tillie.

"Simply wonderful! That is most definitely the idea," said the Admiral, as he took off his hat and threw it into the air!

"Can I please have my Absolutely Genuine Gold Star now?" said Tillie, with her eyes on Willie's gold star.

"Of course, of course, forgive me for not being prompt about the matter," said the Admiral, as the hat landed back on his head. He quickly brought out another Absolutely Genuine Gold Star from under his sleeve and pinned it on the front of Tillie's lab coat pocket.

"Very well," said the Admiral. "Let us go onward and backward to my Heroical Storical Laboratory where we shall endeavor to practice the skills of a Heroical-Storical-Observicorical-Researchorical-Scientifical-Mate, in our pursuit of heroes who are Character Champions, heroes of good character who are courageous, truthful, persevering, sacrificing and who of course also possess Faith Power."

The Admiral took a very quick step backwards and bumped into the circular wall behind him. It suddenly slid open and revealed a large octagonal room. This eight-sided room looked like both a scientific laboratory and a library. There were four telescopes positioned in four corners and four microscopes sitting on wooden tables. Floor to ceiling bookshelves filled half the room and held more books than Willie or Tillie could count. They were arranged in a pattern like sections of an orange. From where they were standing, the twins could see two neatly hand painted signs, one on the end of the closest bookshelf and one on the end of the farthest bookshelf.

The first read:

Books are mysterious—some filled with wisdom, some filled with facts, and some filled with hope. Read a good book, fill your mind with wonder, feel your mind expand, and like a muscle your mind will be strengthened and stretched . . . watch it learn and grow.

*   —Author unknown*

The second sign read:

The more you read, the more you know—The more you know, the smarter you grow—The smarter you are, the stronger your voice— When speaking your mind or making your choice.

*   —Author unknown*

In the middle of the room sat a large over-stuffed high-backed chair and two ottomans (round cushioned stools). The chair and ottomans rested on a large rug that had a complete map of the solar system carefully stitched in its fabric.

The group entered the unusual room. They were greeted by a crackling fire and the delicious smell of hot chocolate.

"Mates, do sit down and make yourselves comfortable," said the Admiral. "The Captain will be quick to serve you one of the finest mugs of hot chocolate you will ever have the pleasure to enjoy, from our very own Hotchocolatematic."

The Captain left the Admiral's shoulder and flew over to a very large brass machine with all sorts of pipes shooting out of it, some in wild loops and some pointing straight up. Steam came out of some and boiling and gurgling noises could be heard from the others.

"How's the Captain going to get hot chocolate from that?" asked Tillie as she stared straight at the odd contraption, which was almost the size of a refrigerator.

"Remember, mates, your expectation can be wrong about something," said the Admiral, who spoke with a slight annoyance. He didn't appreciate lack of faith or belief in any of his abilities or creations. "Expectations can be quite a bother—better to set them aside and let surprise come your way!"

The Captain motioned to Willie to come over. Willie very excitedly stepped forward to try the machine. "Tell the Hotchocolatematic what you want," said the Captain.

Willie had no doubt that the unusual Hotchocolatematic would give him what he asked, so he boldly presented his request: "Please, may I have a mug of the finest tasting hot chocolate, with whipped cream and choco-late sprinkles on top?"

At the sound of Willie's voice, the machine suddenly made a whirring noise, and then a white enameled spigot popped out from its side. A door slid open and a small tray with a red dotted mug on it slid out underneath the spigot with a whining noise. The spigot opened by itself and began to pour out the richest, steamiest hot chocolate Willie had ever seen. All this time the bubbling and gurgling sounds got louder and a grinding noise could be heard. Finally, there was a sucking sound, and out of the spigot came the biggest glop of whipped cream and chocolate sprinkles that Willie had ever imagined on a mug of hot chocolate. The big mug was almost the size of Willie's head, but he was strong, so he was able to pick it up. As he did, the small tray slid quietly back into the machine. Willie was quite astonished and pleased!

Tillie suddenly decided that she wanted a big mug of hot chocolate, too, because she simply couldn't wait one more second, after seeing Willie's mug and smelling the hot chocolate.

"I want a mug of hot chocolate, too! I want it now! And I want it with more whipped cream than my brother has," shouted Tillie. The jolly bubbling gurgling noises stopped, and the small door on the side slid shut. Tillie looked at the machine for a moment, and a very sour frown formed on her face. The Hotchocolatematic suddenly became quiet.

"What's going on?" said Tillie, feeling quite unhappy. "This ridiculous-looking machine is broken."

"The machine is far from broken, dear Tillie," said the Admiral. "It does not respond because it will not hear loud, impolite and impatient demands. The Hotchocolatematic is very, very sensitive. Never rush and demand the mug; it will come to you at the right time. Impatience can often lead to trouble and dis-appointment, dear mates. Remember, patience is a good thing, indeed, which reminds me of an outstanding Character Champion named Daniel Boone."

The Admiral took a deep breath, and thoughtfully stroked his mustache. "Yes, Daniel Boone was an outstanding Character Champion, because he was patient, courageous, honest and persevering. Persevering means that he never gave up when trials and troubles came along. Daniel tried to do well and right even at times when everything around him was falling apart. One of his brothers and two of his sons lost their lives in battles with the Shawnee people and, when he was older, he lost over one hundred thousand acres of his Kentucky land because of dishonest lawyers and their legal arguments. You shall hear more about this soon."

"I didn't know Daniel Boone had sadness and problems in his life," said Willie. "I thought heroes always won and never failed at anything."

"Ah, well," said the Admiral. "They are winners, it is true, but it is in the overcoming of the big problem and the discouragement that makes the hero a true Character Champion."

"Daniel Boone was indeed an overcomer," said the Captain. "Heroes don't win every battle or get everything they want. Heroism is seen in what characters overcome as they do their best for good, truth and right, no matter what problems happen." The Captain stood still, as if at attention.

"Daniel overcame many obstacles by persevering with Faith Power and courage, as true Character Champions always do," finished the Admiral.

"Well, I know all about Daniel Boone," said Tillie with a flip of her ponytail. "My research report is already done."

Willie didn't say anything. He knew his report wasn't done, and he felt embarrassed and a tad ashamed that he had already decided that heroes, history, and he would part ways.

Before Tillie could say anything else, the Captain began to sing a silly ditty:

We don't know all there is to know,
And what we think we know isn't always so.
The wise know how much they don't know,
And that's the way it goes.

"I could not have sung it better myself," said the Admiral, "and you are precisely correct, of course. Captain, do get Tillie a big mug of my finest hot chocolate with a very large glop of whipped cream, and do not neglect the chocolate sprinkles."

Tillie soon had a very big steaming mug of hot chocolate and both mates followed the Captain and Admiral to the chair and the two round ottomans. Willie and Tillie sat on the ottomans, the Admiral sat on the overstuffed high-backed chair, and the Captain perched on the arm of the chair. He pulled out another cracker and began to munch on it.

The Admiral put his hand to his chest and straightened up, looking very serious and important. "Hear, hear! Cheers to Willie and Tillie for wanting to learn and grow, and might I add, if one is not learning and growing, then what are they doing? Now, please raise your mugs high and toast the amazing Daniel Boone and the great virtues of patience and perseverance for which he was known! You will be hearing more about these fine and wonderful character traits before long."

Willie and Tillie lifted their big mugs high (it took both of their hands to lift them up), and gladly toasted Daniel Boone and the great virtues and wonderful character traits they really didn't understand.

"Excellent, mates. Now that we are all comfortable, and made so by a bit of refreshment, let us begin the Heroical Storical," said the Admiral.

"I can't wait to hear the Daniel Boone storical," said Willie.

Tillie glanced at her brother and suddenly blurted out, "You have a whipped-cream mustache!"

Willie quickly brushed the whipped-cream mustache from his lip.

"Never mind, Willie, I have had one or two myself," said the Admiral, chuckling to himself. "Dare I say, Tillie, dear, you have a chocolate sprinkle on your front tooth. Now let us continue, mates, and not forget that flaws and imperfections are not far from any of us...The wise character understands this fact. Now, where should we begin...hmm..." He paused and again stroked his mustache. "Tillie, you asked about my collectibles...those wonder-filled collectibles..."

The Captain also looked very serious and stroked his beard.

The Admiral's face brightened as he

thought of an idea. The Captain's face quickly brightened, too.

"Collectibles are clues to knowledge and understanding which will lead us to the telling of the Heroical Storical," said the Admiral. "Indeed, mates, I have a collectible or two from Daniel Boone's life."

The Admiral reached deep into his pocket and again brought out his key ring with the one hundred petite sized keys. "Finding the key to my over-stuffed trunk will be a challenge. But without a challenge one's true character cannot be known."

The Admiral held the key ring close to his face. He squinted at the different keys. Finally, he pulled out a monocle from his coat pocket and began to examine the keys, one by one. "Yes, excellent," he loudly announced, "here is the key."

"How do you know?" asked Willie.

"An excellent question, indeed," said the

Admiral, beaming at Willie. "We should always ask that question about anything we are told! I happen to know that this is the key because here in very fine letters, that only I can see with my monocle, are the words, 'This is the key to the trunk.'"

"Can I see the letters?" asked Tillie.

"Why, certainly," said the Admiral, as he let Tillie see through the monocle. "You should always check and verify what someone tells you if you can, even if it is my word you are checking and verifying," he said with a chuckle.

The Captain flew off the arm of the chair and onto the shoulder of the Admiral. "I've never known him to be wrong," he said. "After all, his name is Wright and not Wrong!" The Captain burst out laughing, very satisfied with his joke.

Chapter Five

The Heroical Storical
Almost Begins

The Admiral put away his monocle. Then he reached down and unlocked the trunk with the small key. Tillie quickly reached into the trunk and grabbed the first thing she touched. She brought out a bent bugle.

"This doesn't look special or valuable," she said as she looked at it.

"I think it does," said Willie.

"Slow down, mates," said the Admiral, as he took the bugle from Tillie. "Each wonder-filled collectible in my trunk has a fascinating, incredible and very factual story behind it, and such a collectible, more times than not, reveals the courage and heroism of the one who owned it. This bugle, for your amazement and enlightenment, belonged to none other than General Robert E. Lee, who blew it at the Battle of Bull Run. He blew it as a call to arms for his outnumbered army as they faced enemy soldiers closing in on them from all sides."

Willie excitedly grabbed the bugle out of the Admiral's hands. He put the bugle to his lips and gave it a long loud blast, blowing Captain Perry right off his perch! The surprised Captain fluttered to the floor and landed with a thump.

"Ouch, mate!" said the Captain as he rubbed his head.

"Are you hurt?" asked Willie.

"I've had worse, mate," said the Captain, as he tried to smooth his ruffled feathers. "But that was quite a gale force blast!"

"What's this?" asked Tillie, as she reached

into the trunk again and pulled out a rusty candleholder.

"That, Tillie," the Admiral responded, "once belonged to Florence Nightingale. She was a nurse during the Crimean War. At night she would visit the wounded and sick, and they always saw her coming, because she carried a candle to light her way."

"I've heard of her!" said Tillie.

"But today, we are going to hear about Daniel Boone, frontiersman, pioneer trailblazer, explorer, hunter, and most indomitable, indubitable Character Champion!" exclaimed the Admiral, as he brought out from the trunk a wide brimmed hat with a small bullet sized hole in the front part of the brim.

"What do those words mean?" Willie asked.

"Indomitable means unbeatable, silly," said Tillie with a flip of her ponytail. "And indubitable means honest."

"May I correct you, Tillie, dear?" the Admiral said with a small smile. "Something that is indubitable is simply without question. Something that is surefire and certain could be described as indubitable."

The Admiral took his hat off his head and carefully placed the wide-brimmed hat on his head with the hole facing forward. "Hmm, this hat appears heavier than usual," he said. The hat moved back and forth and suddenly began to rise up.

Willie and Tillie began to laugh. "It's Captain Perry Parrot, he's under your hat," said Willie.

The Captain's beak poked through the hole. "That's right mates, it's me! I've been known to get into an odd place from time to time," he said in a muffled voice.

"Captain Perry Parrot! Indeed!" the Admiral said with a polite chuckle, as he reached up and took the hat off the struggling

Captain. "Your feet have tickled the hairs on my head. How did you get yourself into Boone's hat?"

"Well...uh," the Captain began.

"Never mind," said the Admiral. "It is quite all right." The Captain hopped onto the Admiral's shoulder.

"Why does that hat have a hole in it?" Tillie asked.

The Admiral replied, "The reason Daniel Boone's hat has a hole in it will be clearly understood when I begin to tell that most notable Heroical Storical, 'Daniel Boone and the Battle of Boonesborough' said the Admiral as he continued. I must say, also, that Boone's persevering character during the battle shined like the brilliance of the noon-day sun."

"You mean, he didn't give up?" asked Willie.

"Precisely," said the Admiral. "Indeed, the

Character Champion, Daniel Boone, crashed through many quitting points in that battle, with courage and Faith Power!"

Willie thought for a moment. "Didn't Daniel Boone wear a coonskin cap?"

"I read a book once that said Daniel Boone never wore coonskin caps. It was Davy Crocket!" said Tillie with a smug smile.

"Tillie, you are right about the fact that Daniel Boone never wore coonskin caps. It was said that Boone disdained the uncouth coonskin cap. He chose to wear a Quaker-style hat." The Admiral paused and motioned to Captain Perry, who flew up to a cord dangling from the ceiling. He grabbed it with his beak and pulled, and a large map dropped from the ceiling.

The Admiral continued, "Mates, to help you to understand where the Battle of Boonesborough took place, I have here a fine map of Kentucky from the year 1784, prepared by none other than a schoolteacher from

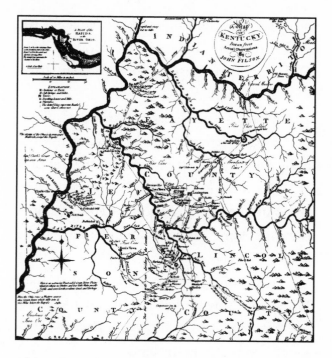

Chester County, Pennsylvania, John Filson. The map is from Filson's book, The Discovery, Settlement and Present state of Kentucke. Filson, a short time later, wrote and published the first book on Boone's adventures, *The Adventures of Col. Daniel Boone*. These facts are important bits of knowledge for you both to store in your Heroical-Storical-Observicorical-Researchorical-Scientifical Knowledge Bank."

"What's a Knowledge Bank?" asked Willie.

"A Knowledge Bank is a place in your brain where you put facts," said the Captain. "It's like a filing cabinet in your head where you can keep information so you can draw out interesting thoughts and ideas when you need to!"

"A Knowledge Bank in my brain?" asked Willie, touching his head. "I like that idea."

"Me, too," said Tillie. "But I already have a lot of knowledge in my bank."

"Remember, Tillie, one can always learn more and put more facts and experience in one's brain," the Admiral said. "Of course, one must want to know for knowledge to grow." He began to sing another silly ditty to the thump of his hand on his armchair rest.

To know one must know that he wants to know.
For learning and wanting to learn makes it so.
Without such desire, one ends up in ire,
For he or she never will learn, know or grow.
If you know that you know,
teach others, like school.
For it is often the mark of the fool
To spout folly, jolly, but he doesn't know
What he does not know and his ignorance shows.

It shows and it grows, from his head to his toes.
But if you have knowledge,
you don't squeal and crow,
You won't get puffed up because you know
How much there could be that you do not know.
Remember this fact, so that you act
And speak with wisdom, in truth, and with tact.
To know is far better than to own fine gold,
For lips that speak knowledge are rare to behold.

The Admiral stood up and took a quick

bow, as the Captain applauded.

"What a ridiculous and silly song!" said Tillie. "I don't get it at all."

"I get it," said Willie. "The Admiral thinks that everyone should learn all they can and not act like they are a big somebody just because they think they know something about something because nobody knows everything about everything."

"Precisely, mate!" The Admiral looked very pleased. "I could not have said it better myself. Congratulations! Here is another Absolutely Genuine Gold Star for you."

The Admiral pulled another star out from under his sleeve and pinned it on Willie's lab coat. Willie couldn't believe it! He had a second gold star!

"Now, mates, look closely at the map," said the Captain, as he reached over and pulled a laser pointer from the Admiral's coat pocket. He flashed the red light on the map. "Here is the famous Wilderness Road."

"I'd like to go on that Wilderness Road," said Willie.

"And I'd like to stop at one of the streams to gather stones," said Tillie.

"The land in Kentucky was very beautiful, and it could take your breath away," said the Admiral. "Daniel Boone, more than any one else, explored and scouted the land of Kentucky, risking his life to make it possible for settlers to move there. He often had to clear land with his own hands, build the first road to it and defend it against the Shawnee, who already lived there and did not like the white men using their hunting grounds. Boone hoped, with all his heart, that these native tribes could live together in peace with the white settlers in the Kentucky lands, but often-times no treaty or agreement could be reached and kept. Both sides were intent on having their way, and, tragically, war would break out from time to time, causing many people to lose their lives. Daniel did everything he could to keep peace, but this was not always possible."

"Daniel knew not to judge a man by the color of his feathers or skin, but to judge the man by his actions, whether they were good or not so good," said Captain Perry. He dug into the Admiral's trunk for a moment, and then pulled out a large, brightly colored feathered headdress.

"What are you doing with that?" asked Willie.

"I'm just trying on a few new feathers!" the Captain replied, as he put the large headdress on.

"Those feathers are too colorful and they don't match with your green feathers. You look silly and foolish," said Tillie.

"Arrrr, matey, stop right there!" the Captain replied, slightly annoyed. "I just said that Daniel Boone didn't judge by the color of skin, but you're criticizing the color of my feathers! Daniel Boone knew not to judge anyone from their appearance or the things they owned. He never looked down on a settler who was not wearing the latest frontier fashion, nor did he look down on a settler that did not have glass-paned windows in their cabin."

"The Captain is absolutely right, Tillie dear," added the Admiral. "A Merriweather Mate like you would do well to learn the same attitude." The Admiral reached in his pocket for something to eat and found a crumpet. "Always remember, mates, that before someone is qualified to judge another person's character, he or she must judge himself or herself first. I must not forget to mention, as the Captain already has, that someone's character, whether good or bad, must be determined by actions and not by words alone. Individuals with any kind of character can certainly say one thing and do something very different. We learn much more about someone's character from how they act than from what they say. You might want to jot this very important bit of wisdom down on your observation pads."

"I want Daniel Boone to be my friend," said Willie. "He wouldn't tease me if I came to school late and forgot my raincoat. He wouldn't shoot spitballs at me like Billy Bones does at school. Billy shoots spitballs at me because he thinks I talk funny, and he doesn't like anyone that doesn't sound like him."

"Billy Bones shoots spitballs at you because you're an easy target on the dunce stool and you're there because you desk fish and don't pay attention to Miss Dullywinkle's interesting and excellent readings, like I do!" snapped Tillie.

Tillie was preparing for another blast at Willie, who had wandered over to the map and began to study it. He wanted to ignore his sister, but he couldn't. Her words were like stinging nettles in his ears. "You also don't get your schoolwork done on time, especially your RESEARCH REPORTS!"

Admiral Wright sat up straight in his chair and quickly interrupted Tillie, "I must insist that you stop your silly Tillie tirade. Willie's behavior at school is not your problem. It is always best to mind one's own actions. If you are truly doing so, you will have plenty to 'mind' with no time to 'mind' anyone else's business. Being a busybody buzzing in someone's faults and weaknesses, even if it is your own twin brother's, is not a wise expenditure of your effort and time."

Willie, with a slight smile, turned to look at his sister who gave him an exasperated frown. She couldn't understand why her brother just wouldn't do things her way, and she also couldn't understand how he always managed to come out ahead.

"Shall we proceed?" asked the Admiral as

he took a bite from his crumpet. "Daniel Boone was a friend to everyone, including many of the Shawnee, whom he considered at the end of his life to be some of the best friends he ever had. Daniel owed his skills as an expert hunter, tracker and explorer to some of the Delawares, or otherwise known as 'Lenape' in their own language. The Shawnees also taught Daniel important survival skills when he was a young boy in the Pennsylvania woods."

Willie continued to study the old map carefully. He was soon joined by Tillie, who was curious too, and when she did, she suddenly shouted (as if she had discovered the cure for polio) "Boonesborough is named after Daniel Boone."

"Outstanding, Tillie, a good deduction!" said the Admiral. "That kind of thinking is what I expect from a true Heroical-Storical-Observicorical-Researchorical-Scientifical-Mate! Boonesborough was named after Daniel

Boone because he was admired for his leadership skills and courage by many of the settlers in Kentucky. Of course, no matter how noble one is, there are always some who will criticize and find fault. Later in his life, Daniel experienced severe criticism from some very clever and not so nice lawyers who wrongfully claimed that Daniel was not entitled to his Kentucky land. They forcefully argued in court against Daniel, saying that he had not properly filed the correct legal papers to secure his property. Sadly, the lawyers won, and Daniel lost all of the land he had claimed and settled."

"That's not fair," said Tillie.

"It certainly seems that way," the Admiral replied. "Daniel chose not to become bitter about his loss of land. Instead, he moved into a new area, which is now Missouri. The Spanish government controlled that area during that period of history, and they granted Daniel Boone a large portion of land. You see, mates, Daniel Boone was a character who didn't hold grudges. He knew how to forgive. Even though his son had been murdered, he still tried to build friendship bridges with the tribes. He understood how they felt about white men taking over their lands, and he tried to work for peace between the groups of settlers and native tribes. This was not always possible, because there were some settlers and Shawnees who were too angry to try and settle their differences peacefully."

"Do you remember who Daniel's best friends were when he was a small boy?" asked the Captain. "I'm just testing whether you're making deposits into your Knowledge Bank." The Captain began munching on a celery stick.

"I remember!" shouted Willie as he leaped up and almost knocked the Captain's celery stick from his beak. "Daniel's boyhood buddies were some of the Delawares and Shawnees. They shared their expert frontier survival skills with him."

"Absolutely right," said the Captain, as he began to spread some peanut butter on his celery stick.

"I could never be friends with any group that was responsible for hurting my children," said Tillie.

"Daniel could," said the Admiral. "It takes courage and faith to forgive and move on, and the fact that he did is one of the reasons that he is a perfect candidate for my Admiral Wright's Heroes' Great Wall of Faith. Daniel could understand what it was like to lose loved ones, so he felt sorry that many of his tribal friends also suffered the loss of their children, friends, and other family members in battles with the settlers."

"Aye, war is a terrible, horrible occurrence," said the Captain in a very serious voice.

"Captain, you have a tear in your eye," said Tillie. "Be careful not to rub your eyes because you might get some of your peanut butter in them."

The Captain brought out a handkerchief. "Excuse me, mates. I can get a bit choked up when I think about the loss of lives on both sides." The Captain then used the handkerchief to blow his beak. "Don't worry about peanut butter getting in my eyes. I have mastered the art of spreading it on my celery sticks without getting any on my wing tips. So now when I rub my eyes I won't have my old 'peanut butter in the eye' problem."

"Indeed, it is very sad when one thinks of the loss of lives because of anger, hate and disagreements," said the Admiral, as he turned to look at the Captain. "It can also be a difficult experience when one gets peanut butter in one's eye. It certainly has been somewhat of a serious problem for the Captain, but now it seems the Captain has indeed triumphed in his struggle to master the skill of spreading peanut butter on his celery stick without getting any on his wing tips.

"Moving on, mates," the Admiral said as he gave the Captain a light pat on the back, "I believe that Daniel Boone had one of his fiercest tests of courage, patience, bravery and perseverance at the Battle of Boonesborough.

"I also believe that now would be a perfect time for a cup of my very favorite peppermint tea and, of course, my very furry slippers. I must have them before I can fully undertake the telling of the story of the Battle of Boonesborough. If it is not too much trouble, Captain, I shall hold your celery stick if you would be so kind as to bring them to me.

"Crumpets can be a bit dry, you know," he said to Willie and Tillie, as the Captain flew off.

The Captain quickly returned with two very furry slippers and a cup of hot, steaming tea. A lovely peppermint aroma filled the air.

"Greatly appreciated," said the Admiral, as he handed the celery stick back to the Captain.

The Admiral placed his feet in the very furry slippers, and took a long sip of his very favorite peppermint tea.

Chapter Six

The Heroical Storical
Actually Begins

Admiral Wright put his teacup down, cleared his throat and began. "The Battle of Boonesborough is a most noted Heroical Storical from Daniel Boone's life. It has its start with the capture of Daniel Boone by the Shawnee Warriors. Let me explain, and I will begin now." He cleared his throat again.

"Oh, please do, we can't wait any longer!" said Willie and Tillie, at the same time. They looked at each other, surprised that their words matched perfectly!

The Admiral leaned forward in his chair, lowered his voice and looked into the eyes of Willie and Tillie. The Admiral didn't want the mates to miss one single word. "It was the eighth day of January in the year 1778 when Daniel Boone and thirty men packed their horses loaded with iron kettles, and left Boonesborough, Kentucky. They were headed for the Lower Blue Licks to get salt for the settlement. Salt was important to the settlement as it was used as a preservative for meat. Collecting salt was very hard work. Eight hundred and forty gallons of salt water had to be boiled down to produce just one bushel of salt! Daniel's men set up camp and worked long hours in the day, collecting brine, chopping wood, tending the fires, and scraping salt from the kettles."

"Arrr! Sailing upon the briny sea! The salty sea is the life for me!" said the Captain, hopping on one leg like Long John Silver from *Treasure*

Island.

The Admiral gave him a slight frown, annoyed by the interruption, and continued. "By February, Daniel's men were nearly finished with their salt collecting, and had been producing about ten bushels of salt a day.

"On one very cold and snowy February day, while the other men were making salt, Daniel left the group to go hunting alone. At the end of his hunt, Daniel decided to return to camp. He was on foot, leading his horse which was loaded with three to four hundred pounds of fresh buffalo meat. As he traveled through the dark snowy forest, he suddenly sensed danger. He heard a crackle in the brush and, quickly turning, saw the shapes of Shawnee warriors through the falling snow. Daniel needed to make a quick escape! He wanted to jump on his horse and ride off, but he had a problem. He could not dump all the buffalo meat—the leather straps that held the meat were frozen stiff. He had to face the not so friendly warriors surrounding him, and he couldn't speed away on his horse."

"I'd have unbuckled the saddle, dumped

the buffalo meat and rode bareback to get away fast," said Willie.

"The buckles would have been frozen stiff, too," said Tillie.

"Good thinking Tillie, that was exactly the problem!" said the Admiral. "All Daniel could do was abandon his horse and run as fast as possible. Unfortunately, he was not fast enough, because the young warriors caught up with him within half a mile. Daniel knew that he could not escape, so he leaned his rifle against a tree, which meant he was willing to give up without a fight. The Shawnee took him to Chief Blackfish's camp, three miles away.

"At the camp, Daniel was surprised to see one hundred and twenty warriors decorated with war paint in the middle of the winter. He knew that the Shawnee seldom went to war during the cold winter months. Daniel soon realized that the reason the warriors were on the warpath was for a big surprise attack on

Boonesborough. He realized that if he was going to be able to help the men and their families staying there, he would have to act very carefully. The lives of every person in Boonesborough, including Daniel's, were in danger. He looked around carefully at all the painted faces and saw someone he recognized. Daniel Boone was a friendly sort of chap, so he greeted his old acquaintance quite enthusiastically, 'Howdy do, Captain Will!' Captain Will was a Shawnee warrior who had captured and robbed him and his friend, Stewart, eight years earlier in Kentucky. Daniel acted pleased to be with the Shawnee, and reached out to shake his hand. Captain Will laughed and shook his hand. When they realized that Daniel was not afraid and was even friendly, all the other tribal members stood around and shook his hand, too. He was friendly with these people who could have been his enemies. He understood that it was always in the best interest of everyone if one deals with enemies with great diplomacy and wisdom."

"Diplomacy? What's that?" asked Willie.

"Diplomacy is the skill of being able to solve problems without getting into ugly and destructive fights which can lead to war and loss of lives." said Captain Perry.

"I would have been very scared to be made a prisoner," said Tillie.

"Well, Daniel wasn't easily frightened," said the Captain. "Besides, his desire to do what was right forced him to face and conquer his fear. That's why he was able to treat a hostile group with respect and fairness."

"That is exactly the point I am getting to," the Admiral continued. "Chief Blackfish asked Daniel about the other men in his group, and Daniel told him that they had remained behind at the salt lick. Blackfish then told Daniel that the warriors were on their way to destroy Boonesborough as retaliation for the death of Cornstalk, a Shawnee chief."

"What does 'retaliation' mean?" asked Willie.

"Retaliation means to 'get even,' as you say, with someone who does something to you that you don't like," responded the Admiral. "Chief Blackfish was angry over the death of his friend, Chief Cornstalk, who had done everything he could to peacefully settle the problems between the white settlers and the Shawnee. Three months earlier, in November, Cornstalk had gone to the American commander at Point Pleasant on the Ohio River to discuss peace. Sadly, Cornstalk and the other Shawnee were thrown into a prison and later killed by a group of frontiersmen."

"Well, I'd be very angry, too!" said Willie.

"It is never right to mistreat and cruelly hurt others, no matter how much they disagree with you or are different from you," said the Admiral.

"That's right," added the Captain, looking very serious and stroking his beard.

"Daniel must have felt very badly about what happened to Chief Cornstalk and his tribesmen," said Tillie.

"Indeed, Daniel did feel badly. He hated senseless killing of any kind," said the Admiral.

"While standing in the clearing with Captain Will and the rest of the Shawnees, Daniel tried to think fast and come up with a peaceful solution," continued the Admiral. "He came up with the following good idea." He told Chief Blackfish that he would convince his men to give up without fighting if Blackfish would wait until spring to make his attack on Boonesborough. By then, Daniel said, he would be able to talk the other frontier folks at the settlement into surrendering as well. Daniel reminded the Chief of the hardships of winter warfare, such as the simple fact of the scarcity of food during the cold winter months. If the Shawnees were on the warpath, they would not be able to hunt as they normally would. Daniel's diplomatic skills worked—Chief Blackfish agreed. He decided that Daniel's men at the salt lick would not be harmed as long as they surrendered to Chief Blackfish and his warriors.

"The next day, Daniel Boone, Chief Blackfish and the Shawnee warriors arrived at Blue Licks. Two of Daniel's men, Flanders Callaway and Thomas Brooks, were not at the camp when Daniel arrived with the warriors. When Daniel's men saw the Shawnee warriors they grabbed their guns, but Daniel shouted, 'Don't fire! If you do we will be massacred!' The men laid down their guns and allowed the Shawnee warriors to capture them.

"Blackfish had promised that Daniel and his men would not be hurt, but many of his warriors were not happy with this decision.

They wanted to kill Boone and his men. To deal with the situation diplomatically, Blackfish called a council and invited Daniel to join in. Hours went by, as Shawnee after Shawnee spoke either for or against ending the lives of Daniel and his friends.

"Finally, Blackfish gave Daniel an opportunity to speak to defend his life and the lives of the other prisoners. Daniel stood up and looked each warrior in the eye. He bravely told them, 'Don't kill us, for we'll be of use to you as warriors and hunters. We'll work for you and help provide for the women and children.'"

"Did Daniel's speech save his life?" asked Willie.

"Of course it did," said Tillie. "If it didn't, the Admiral wouldn't have a Heroical Storical to tell us about the Battle of Boonesborough."

The Admiral continued. "The final vote was sixty-one to fifty-nine to spare the lives of Daniel Boone and his men."

"Whew," said the Captain. "That was close! I would have been shaking in my feathers if I were waiting for a bunch of Shawnee Warriors to vote whether I should live or die!"

"Yeah, me too!" said Willie.

"You don't have feathers," said Tillie.

"What happened next?" asked Willie.

Admiral Wright took a long sip of his peppermint tea and began again. "Blackfish planned to take Daniel and his men to Chillicothe, a small Shawnee town on the banks of the Little Miami River in Ohio country."

"Look here on the map," said Captain Perry, who used a red laser pointer to indicate the location of the Miami River.

"I see the town, 'Chillicothe,'" said Tillie.

"The Shawnees and their prisoners were not going to go to Chillicothe until the next day, so they made Daniel run the gauntlet that night," said the Admiral.

"What's the gauntlet?" asked Willie.

"I was hoping you would ask me that," replied the Admiral. "The gauntlet was a tribal custom, a kind of greeting put on for the entertainment and amusement of the tribes. When prisoners were taken, a whole village, including the women and children, would stand in two parallel lines, with antlers, bats, poles, sticks and rocks to beat and injure the prisoners, who were made to run between the lines, from one end to the other. Those who were not bold or strong enough to run quickly ended up dying while trying to complete the run. Many prisoners died when running the gauntlet. This was what Daniel was made to face."

"That sure doesn't sound like a very fun greeting!" said Willie.

"It wasn't about fun; the gauntlet was a big test of the courage and stamina of a person," said the Captain. "Those who passed lived and those who didn't died. It was that simple."

"It sounds scary!" said Tillie.

The Admiral continued. "Blackfish promised that he would not harm the prisoners, but told Daniel that he was not included in the promise. Daniel would, most definitely, have to prove himself strong. If not, he would die."

"That's not fair," said Tillie.

"The decision to make Daniel run the gauntlet had nothing to do with fairness," said the Admiral. "Daniel had no choice but to face the challenge and pray that he would make it out alive. He looked up to heaven and prayed. He needed Faith Power to give him courage, strength, speed, agility and perseverance to run the race and win!

"Daniel began the gauntlet, as the Shawnees held sticks and clubs. They formed two lines, and Boone was forced to run between them. He was quick like a deer, running for his life! Daniel knew that if he fell, he would be clubbed to death.

"Boone later told a grandson, 'I set out full

speed, first running so near one line that they could not do me much damage, and when they give back, I crossed over to the other side, and by that means was likely to pass through without much hurt.'"

"Daniel did a zigzag run!" said Willie.

"Correct," said the Admiral. "Daniel zigzagged back and forth to each side of the line in order to survive the grueling gauntlet. As he neared the end, one of the Shawnees stepped into his path to deliberately block him from completing the gauntlet. Daniel, later in his life, said, 'The only way to avoid meeting the warrior's club was to run over him by springing at him with my head bent forward, taking him full in the chest, and sending him flat on his back, so I would pass over him unhurt.' Boone did exactly that and cheers went up from both Daniel's group and the Shawnee who crowded around him. Thus, Daniel impressed his captors and won their respect.

The Shawnee shook Daniel's hands and slapped him on the back while congratulating him for his victory. Daniel looked up and gave a small nod to heaven, giving the victory to a bigger Someone. Daniel's mother had taught him as a small boy to believe in God, the Creator of everyone and everything, and to go to Him when strength, wisdom and courage were needed to face big battles or problems."

"Whew, I'm tired just thinking about how exhausted Daniel must have been after he finished his race," said the Captain as he stretched his wings back—and fell backwards into the Admiral's teacup! He landed bottom down with both of his feet hanging over the teacup's edge!

"Oh, frazzled feathers!" he spluttered. "Excuse me!" He felt quite embarrassed as he struggled to get out of the cup. "My plan was not to take a bath in your cup of tea, Admiral. Forgive me, if you please!"

"Quite all right. May I give you a hand?" the Admiral said, as he took hold of the Captain's wing tip and carefully helped him out of the cup.

"Thanks, Admiral," said the Captain, as he began to flutter his wings to dry them.

"Don't worry about it; you'll dry fast," said Willie.

"I found something to help you dry off," said Tillie as she handed him a small white cloth.

"Very well, now that the Captain has made a bit of a splash, shall we move on?" asked the Admiral. "Now, where were we?" The Admiral looked thoughtful and stroked his mustache.

"The gauntlet," said Tillie.

"Yes, the gauntlet," said the Admiral. "The morning following the gauntlet, Chief Blackfish and his tribe set out for Chillicothe with Daniel and his men, which was a march of one hundred miles. They walked for ten days in the snow, and there was little food. Daniel told everyone to chew the bark of the slippery elm and eat the sap oozing from the white oak trees."

"Yuck, I wouldn't have liked that," said Tillie.

"I would," said Willie.

"When they finally arrived at Chillicothe, a few dozen Shawnees, including women and children, greeted the group," the Admiral continued. "Chief Blackfish and the Shawnees there made a decision to adopt Daniel and some of his men into their tribe to replace members of their families who had died in battle. Daniel and some of his men agreed, knowing that they would likely get better treatment. As for the men who were not adopted, many of them were quite unpleasant and very grumpy, so much so that the Shawnee had to decide whether they should even be allowed to remain in the village. These grumpy men became so disagreeable that Chief Blackfish finally decided to deliver them to the British at Fort Detroit.

"Meanwhile, Daniel, unlike the grumpy men, tried to be cheerful, in spite of the trying situation, and the Shawnees were appreciative of his cheerfulness. Chief Blackfish not only appreciated his good nature, but he also respected Daniel's integrity and strength. He decided he wanted Daniel Boone to be his own adopted son."

"Admiral, I know what's coming next," said the Captain, pulling a feather from his head while he continued. "May I tell the Heroical Storical now?"

"Why, you may, of course," said the Admiral, as he leaned back into his chair to relax and added, "Do tell the mates about Boone's big scrub, a very important bath for a very dirty frontiersman!"

"Of course I will tell the mates about

Daniel's big scrub," said the Captain, as he pulled another feather from his head while he continued. "Blackfish ordered Boone to be taken to the river, and scrubbed head to foot by squaws."

"Squaws?" asked Willie.

"Squaws were the married women of the tribe, women who knew the skills and crafts of the Shawnee," said the Captain. "They scrubbed him hard with lots of soap and water. Those frontiersmen didn't have showers, and didn't have too much time to bathe. So you can guess that Daniel Boone was pretty dirty! The squaws then pulled out all of Daniel's hair, except for a three-inch tuft on top of his head. They also decorated Daniel's scalp with beads and feathers."

"Exactly correct, and a fine telling, Captain," said the Admiral. "Do go on."

"Thank you, Admiral," continued the Captain. "After Daniel was feathered and beaded, he was officially made a Shawnee at a ceremony at the council house. Boone was considered a true Shawnee now, and given a new name, Sheltowee, which meant 'Big Turtle.'"

"Daniel's head must have been pretty sore, after those squaws pulled out his hair!" said Tillie. "How does your head feel, Captain, after your feather plucking?"

The Captain rubbed his head and began to eat another cracker. "Not bad at all," he said.

"I would have felt stupid wearing all the girlish beads and feathers," said Willie.

"Whether or not Daniel felt stupid, he was grateful to be alive," said the Admiral. "Gratitude, however, did not prevent him from looking for a way to escape during the four months of living with the Shawnees. He missed his real family and wanted to go home. Not only that, dear mates, but he wanted to protect Boonesborough from the possible attack."

"Whatever happened to Daniel's men, Flanders Callaway and Thomas Brooks?" asked Tillie. "I wrote their names down on my observation pad because they were not there when Chief Blackfish and the warriors came to the salt licks."

"Excellent question, Tillie," the Admiral replied.

"Those observation pads are very handy," said the Captain.

The Admiral leaned forward in his chair. "You rightly note that not all of Daniel's men were captured at the Blue Licks when the Shawnee arrived," he continued, "Callaway and Brooks were out hunting when the Shawnee warriors came to capture Daniel's men. After they left, and Callaway and Brooks came back to camp, they knew that the Shawnees had kidnapped Daniel and the other men."

"How did they know?" asked Willie.

"Another good question," said the

Admiral. "You are really thinking like a true Heroical-Storical-Observicorical-Researchorical-Scientifical-Mate! Callaway and Brooks knew that the Shawnees had been there because of the clues that were left behind: feathers, signs of a scuffle, and broken branches. Daniel's men remembered that the Shawnee lived in the area so they reasoned rightly that they were the tribe responsible for kidnapping Daniel. Later, another group of men from Boonesborough arrived which was supposed to relieve the salt workers. When Callaway and Brooks told them that Daniel and his men had been kidnapped, all the men together decided to follow the trail of the Shawnee to the Ohio River, hoping to rescue them. After searching, they did not find Daniel, so the group returned to Boonesborough with the bad news that Daniel and his men had been captured by the Shawnees."

"Did Daniel have a wife waiting for him at

Boonesborough?" asked Tillie.

"Indeed he did," said the Admiral. "Daniel's wife was a fine, hardworking woman named Rebecca, who bore him ten children. She felt sad after hearing the news about Daniel's kidnapping by the Shawnees. What was worse, she did not know whether she would see her husband alive again. Rebecca decided to leave Boonesborough, because she wanted safety. She took the children with her and went back to her family in North Carolina."

"Well, not all of her children went with her," said the Captain.

"Right you are," said the Admiral. "Her daughter Jemima was married to Flanders Callaway, and she decided to stay in Boonesborough. That way, if her father returned (and she was convinced that he would) she would be there to help him."

"Jemima was a very loyal daughter!" said Tillie.

"Indeed, she was," said the Admiral. "Jemima supported her father more than any of his other daughters. She was very grateful to him for saving her and two other girls from being kidnapped by a small war party made up of two Cherokees and three Shawnees, two years earlier. The great rescue of the girls would make another exciting Heroical Storical! That one will be for another time."

The Captain flew up onto the Admiral's shoulder. "The Admiral has more Heroical Storicals than anyone I know!" he said.

The Admiral stroked his mustache. "Where were we?" He paused, "Oh yes, we took a bit of a side trail, so let us return to the main trail that leads back to the Battle of Boonesborough.

"One month had passed since Boone's capture, and Chief Blackfish decided to go to Fort Detroit to sell the grumpy men in Daniel's group to the British. Remember, mates, the

Shawnees didn't want to adopt grumpy men into their families."

"Good idea," said Tillie.

"Why would the British want grumpy men?" asked Willie.

"Let me explain," the Admiral replied. "The British were not very happy that settlers were moving West. This meant that they could lose control of the area. So they wanted to capture settlers, hoping that other settlers would find out and be discouraged from moving West. Of course, determined and independent settlers like Daniel Boone would not be frightened so easily. Kentucky's beautiful country and abundant wildlife were worth the risk for many."

"Excuse me, Admiral," said the Captain, "but if you don't mind, I would like to tell the Heroical Storical now."

"Of course, if you wish," said the Admiral. "Perfect timing, actually. I would like a sip of my peppermint tea, anyway." He took a sip. He then frowned, and brought out his monocle and peered into the cup. "I see that there is a very small feather here, floating near the surface; left, I suspect, from your unexpected bath."

Captain Perry was no longer as green because he flushed a bit red in the face. He quickly brought the Admiral a fresh cup of tea and flew up to the Admiral's shoulder.

"Jolly good show, Captain Perry!" he said. "My tea was beginning to cool down; and how I dislike tepid tea. Do continue the telling of the Heroical Storical."

The Captain continued: "Right! After a long, cold journey, Blackfish arrived at Fort Detroit in March with Daniel and ten of the grumpy men. Remember, the grumpies were not adopted by any of the Shawnee families and Chief Blackfish only cared about selling them."

"Grumpies? Sounds like guppies," said Willie.

"No," said the Captain, "guppies are small fish, and grumpies are those most miserable men with a terrible case of the crabbies, and I don't mean crustaceans."

"Crusty what?" asked Willie.

"Crabs and lobsters are crustaceans, and they have very hard shells," said Tillie with a flip of her ponytail. "But that's not what he's talking about."

"Do let me continue," said the Captain. "The grumpies were sold for about twenty pounds apiece to Governor Henry Hamilton, a British leader. The governor wanted Daniel, too, and was willing to pay one hundred pounds, but the Chief refused to part with his new son. He was proud of Daniel. Then the Chief, Daniel, and the rest of the warriors returned to Chillicothe. Great feasts were prepared. Everyone ate lots of venison, corn, turkey and crackers."

"Crackers?" Tillie interrupted. "I don't think so."

"Well, you're right, mate. They weren't crackers like the ones I eat. It's more reasonable to assume that the Shawnee prepared corn bread for eating at their feasts. Very good observation, mate, I know that you are thinking like a true..."

"Heroical-Storical-Observicorical-Researchorical-Scientifical-Mate!" shouted Willie, who felt very pleased that he had now mastered the pronunciation of the hard-to-say word.

The Captain continued. "Daniel liked his new family. Late in Daniel's life, he told his friends, 'My Shawnee parents were always friendly, sociable and kind.'"

"If I may say so, I am willing to continue the Heroical Storical," said the Admiral.

"Of course, of course," said the Captain.

"I must admit, you are almost as good at expounding and expostulation as I am," said the Admiral, with a chuckle, as he leaned back in his chair and began.

"As much as Daniel liked his adoptive family, he wanted to be with his own wife and children. He missed them very much. He also wanted to escape because he was concerned for the settlers at Boonesborough. The Shawnees were determined to carry out their plan of attack, and Daniel wanted to warn the settlers and help them make the necessary preparations to defend themselves.

"During the four months that Daniel lived with Chief Blackfish as his son, he remained relaxed and friendly with them. Even though Daniel knew of the plans to attack Boonesborough, he was casual and even joked with them at times. On one occasion, Daniel was cleaning their guns, and was able to empty their guns of bullets. He then gave the guns back and started to run away as if he were escaping. The Shawnee raised their guns and fired at him, and Daniel jumped into the air, pretending to catch bullets that he had already put in his leather apron. He assured them that he would not try to escape, telling them 'Boone ain't going away.'"

"But Daniel didn't mean it, mates," said the Captain. "He'd made up his mind to escape, and that's exactly what he was about to do!"

"I like Daniel even more now because he liked to play tricks and jokes. He was fun!" said Willie.

"Daniel was fun, and he also had a clever wit that graced his life and saved him many times from being scalped," said the Admiral. "There was another trick that Daniel liked to play. He would take a hunting knife and act as if he was swallowing it and suddenly he would draw it out from his shirt! The Shawnee always laughed when Daniel did that trick."

"So when did he finally escape?" asked Tillie.

"He escaped one morning before sunrise,

on the sixteenth of June in the year 1778," said the Admiral.

"Since Daniel Boone's capture at the Blue Licks on February 8, 1778, he had been with the Shawnees for one hundred and thirty-eight days," said Willie, while rapidly counting back and forth on his fingers. "However it could be one hundred thirty-nine days, if February of 1778 was a leap year and had twenty-nine days instead of twenty-eight."

"Excellent memory on the date of Daniel's capture!" The Admiral beamed. "You've even done your math correctly. Your observation and attention to details has earned you another Absolutely Genuine Gold Star. Willie, you are positively and most definitely on your way to becoming a true Heroical-Storical-Observicorical-Researchorical-Scientifical-Mate." An Absolutely Genuine Gold Star immediately appeared in the hand of the Admiral, and he pinned it on Willie's lab coat next to his two other stars.

"That's not fair!" said Tillie. "Willie has two more Absolutely Genuine Gold Stars than I have. I only have one!"

"You have spoken correctly, dear Tillie," said the Admiral, "but I feel I must add one important bit of advice. It is generally unwise to measure yourself by another's performance and definitely it is never wise to compare yourself to the efforts of one's twin, which correct thinking characters never do!"

"When do I get another Absolutely Genuine Gold Star?" insisted Tillie.

"Let me ponder for a moment or two," said the Admiral, as he rubbed his chin. "Hmm, when did Tillie practice the skills of a Heroical-Storical-Observicorical-Researchorical-Scientifical-Mate?" He stroked his mustache thoughtfully.

"I know," the Captain declared, as he suddenly brought out a drum and banged it to make an important announcement. "Hear ye, hear ye, every ear here open wide to listen! Tillie Venturely correctly remembered that Flanders Callaway and Thomas Brooks were not at the camp when Daniel arrived with the Shawnee Warriors."

"Indeed, the Captain is right!" the Admiral exclaimed. "Tillie, you have exhibited a fine recollection of an important detail and revealed that you are well on your way to becoming a true Heroical-Storical-Observicorical-Researchorical-Scientifical-Mate. Here is an Absolutely Genuine Gold Star for you as well." He quickly pinned the Absolutely Genuine Gold Star on Tillie's lab coat.

"I also made the deduction that Boonesborough was named after Daniel Boone," Tillie declared, "so I deserve another Absolutely Genuine Gold Star! I am quite clever and bright, if I must say so myself!"

"You were correct about Boonesborough

being named after Daniel Boone," said the Admiral as he pinned another Absolutely Genuine Gold Star on Tillie's coat. "You are also clever and bright, but remember that to tell everyone and be proud of the fact is not a wise or humble attitude. Remember, mates, that it is more honorable if someone else sings your praises."

The Captain began to beat on the drum the rhythm of another silly ditty. He began to sing, as the Admiral tapped his toes and slapped his thigh.

Singing one's own praises is easy to do,
But far better someone else to sing them of you.
It's easy to have pride in our most inner parts.
We feel a bitty bit better inside our hearts...
But when those notes come out of the mouth
We may find we don't know what we sing about.
Notes which seemed true now ring so flat.
Shut your ears, or cover them up with your hat!

A wise one says "esteem yourself not,
Don't build a tower to set yourself on top."
It just might teeter and topple,
And then where will you be?
Not singing your own praises, most definitely!

"Not thinking more highly of oneself than one should is a very good thing. When I was young, I would succumb to such an attitude," said the Admiral.

"I've been known to have a fall or two myself, from time to time," said the Captain, rather quietly.

"Like into the teacup," said Willie, laughing.

"A memorable splash. It was, perhaps, one of my biggest," said the Captain, as he looked down and smoothed his feathers.

"Admiral, can we go back to the Heroical Storical?" asked Tillie. "How did Daniel Boone escape from the Shawnees? I was also thinking about why the squaws scrubbed him and plucked his hair before they traveled to Detroit."

"Oh my, oh my!" exclaimed the Admiral. "I am wrong and not right, this time! My order of the events is a bit mixed up! Tillie has made a brilliant observation and asked a most meaningful question! Daniel's scrub bath and hair plucking happened after he returned from Detroit and not before. He became an adopted Shawnee after their return. Do forgive me for such an error.

"Additionally, I must commend your patience with other delays, even though they have been somewhat necessary for making the Heroical Storical as clear as possible. So let us return to the storical and discover more about Daniel Boone and what happened after his escape, and discuss all the surprising and strange events before the Battle of Boonesborough's first shot rang out."

Chapter Seven

Strange Events Before the Battle of Boonesborough

The Admiral cleared his throat and took several sips of tea. Then he sat back in his chair and put on his monocle. "Everything that happens, whether a noteworthy event or an unimportant detail, follows a series of events. In the case of great events, it becomes very important to know what happened before and after. Heroical Storicals are full of great events, and so we learn about why and how they came about, and the Battle of Boonesborough is no exception."

Whipping out a small brown book with a

tattered and worn cover, the Admiral began to read. "Daniel Boone told his biographer, John Filson..."

"What's a biographer?" Willie stopped the Admiral.

"It's someone who writes down the life story of another person," said Captain Perry.

"Right you are, Captain. So, to continue," the Admiral again began to read, "Daniel Boone told his biographer that 'On the sixteenth of June the year 1778, before sunrise, I departed in the most secret manner, and arrived at Boonesborough on the twentieth, after a journey of one hundred and sixty miles; during which I had but one meal.' He escaped from his Shawnee captors on horseback in the early morning hours, riding as fast as his horse would gallop. Finally, the poor animal collapsed from exhaustion. Daniel continued the journey to Boonesborough on foot. He courageously traveled through dark and dangerous forests, over mountains and across rivers and streams. He stopped once to kill a buffalo, and cooked enough meat for only one meal."

"Did you say 'one hundred sixty miles in only four days?' That's incredible!" Willie said.

"Indeed I did," the Admiral responded. "Such an astounding feat is just one of many examples of what perseverance, determination and Faith Power can accomplish. When he finally reached Boonesborough, he was very tired and hungry, yet eager to see his family. Daniel had been away from them for five months. Imagine his disappointment to learn that his wife, Rebecca, had left with the children! He went into his cabin and sat there alone, except for the family cat, which jumped into his lap and curled up."

"That is so sad," said Willie.

"I would have cried," said Tillie.

"Well, at least he had the cat," said Willie.

"Daniel did cry," said the Captain. "He

often shed tears when life was hard and disappointments overwhelmed him. He wasn't afraid of sadness. But he did start to feel better when his oldest daughter, Jemima, rushed into the cabin and gave him a hug. Remember that Jemima had decided to stay at Boonesborough with her husband, Flanders Callaway, to help her father defend the settlement from the Shawnee. Daniel was very glad to receive the support from Jemima and Flanders. He knew he needed as much help as possible, to prepare and ready Boonesborough for the attack which was soon to come."

"Did he know that he would be greatly outnumbered?" asked Tillie (she remembered this from Miss Dullywinkle's readings in class).

"Not yet," the Admiral replied. "When he did, Daniel would discover that he and his group would be facing over four hundred Shawnee warriors that were backed by the British at Fort Detroit."

"How many settlers were in the fort?" asked Tillie.

"As far as I can recall, there were sixty armed men and a dozen women and twenty children," said the Admiral.

"Sixty fighting men against four hundred? If I were Daniel, I would have been running for my life and hiding under whatever cover I could find," said Willie.

"Certainly, Boone had his trepidations," said the Admiral.

"Trepi-what?" asked Willie.

"Trepidation simply means fears," said the Admiral. He took a long sip of tea. "Remember, mates, that in spite of Daniel's trepidations, he always persevered and crashed through his quitting points with Faith Power and courage.

"He went to work soon after arriving at Boonesborough. The fort needed major repairs and strengthening. The stockade had to be rebuilt, which meant Daniel and the men had to repair the sections of wooden spikes that had rotted as well as fill in the gaps of the wall that had not been completed. In addition, he had to strengthen the gate and fortify the corners so that people could use them to shoot at the enemy and see the entire compound. They were like lookout towers. The women went to work molding bullets and preparing bandages."

"I would never make bullets," said Tillie.

"If your life depended on it, you might change your mind," said the Captain.

"Sometimes what we have to do to survive is something we do not like," said the Admiral.

"In Daniel's time there was a lot to be done for one to survive and staying alive was a very big accomplishment back then," added the Captain.

"Women and children also cleared the brush and worked in the cornfields," continued the Admiral. "It was quite a team effort;

men, women and children working together to prepare the fort for the Shawnee attack."

"No one took long naps in the afternoon," finished the Captain. "There was no time." He yawned and stretched his wings back. "Speaking of naps, hearing about all this work is making me tired."

"Don't fall back into the Admiral's teacup," said Tillie.

"No, no, definitely not this time," said the Captain, while straightening up. But before he could catch himself, he lost his balance and fell face first into the Admiral's crumpet.

"Are you hurt?" asked Tillie, as she bent down to help the Captain.

"I'm fine, just fine," said the Captain, as he brushed crumpet crumbs off his beard. "Picking yourself up after a fall builds the spirit of perseverance," he said. "Daniel Boone and I are alike on this point; we brush the crumbs off and move on." He brought out a comb and proceeded to tidy his beard. He always tried to keep it neat and clean.

"Indeed, you are quite alike on that point," said the Admiral. "Brushing off crumbs and moving on is a very honorable and big thing to do. Now, where were we? Oh yes, I remember, Daniel and his men were repairing the stockade and everyone was helping. Daniel also sent messages to nearby forts, asking for reinforcements and between ten and fifteen extra men came. This brought their total to sixty men, as I said.

"Another member of the group who would defend Boonesborough was William Hancock. He and Daniel had been captured by the Shawnee at the same time. On July 17, a month after Daniel had arrived in Boonesborough, some of the settlers heard the faint cry of a man calling for help from the other side of the Kentucky River. Going across in a canoe, Daniel's men found Hancock, the salt maker, without one stitch of clothing on, and unable to walk. He had escaped from Chillicothe on foot, in the middle of the night in his very natural self, and made it almost completely back through thick brush to Boonesborough. The Shawnees had taken his clothes, assuming he would not attempt the escape, but they were wrong. Need I say that Hancock was quite exhausted and certainly ready for a good meal of roasted buffalo! Once Hancock got back some of his strength he told Daniel and the settlers some very bad news."

"What was that?" asked Willie.

The Admiral leaned forward in his chair and lowered his voice. "The Shawnee were on the warpath, determined to destroy Boonesborough and they were already on their way. Hancock had heard a rumor that the British had supplied the Shawnee with four swivel guns and small artillery pieces. Such news was frightening. The Shawnee were planning to lay siege to Boonesborough, which meant that they would not let anyone in or out, so that the settlers would starve. Then, when they were weak enough or surrendered, the Shawnee would kill the men and take the women and children as prisoners. Might I add, mates, that upon hearing such news, Boone immediately sent a letter to Virginia requesting reinforcements. Boone thought that if Hancock was right, additional men and guns were needed to fight the Shawnee and British. However the reinforcements arrived too late."

"In my recollections of the Heroical Storical, I seem to remember that Hancock tried to stir up anger and distrust of Daniel among the settlers," said the Captain. "Didn't he say that Boone was a traitor who had promised to help the Shawnee win Boonesborough?" The Captain flew back up to the Admiral's shoulder.

"That's absolutely correct!" said the

Admiral. "It may be difficult to believe, but Hancock did indeed raise suspicions about Daniel's loyalty. Remember that Daniel had promised the Shawnee that he would deliver Boonesborough to them and convince the settlers not to fight. What Hancock did was to use this fact to get even with Daniel, even though Daniel had not intended to keep his promise at all. Daniel only said that because he was trying to preserve the lives of his family and friends back at Boonesborough. What Hancock did was to tell everyone about the promise Daniel had made, even saying that Daniel had promised to give everything away that was of value, including the women and children."

"Why was Hancock so mean?" asked Tillie.

"Was that 'retaliation'?" asked Willie.

"I see you are using your Knowledge Bank, Willie!" said the Admiral. "You remembered the word. It is important to note, mates, that even though you do what is good and right, you can still make enemies. Daniel Boone had his enemies, too. Hancock stirred up trouble for Boone because he was jealous. The reason was not because Daniel had done something wrong, but because Hancock envied Boone's popularity, leadership and frontier skills."

"Aye, jealousy can be quite cruel," said the Captain. "I make it a habit to not want what another has. It's a very good thing to want what I have and not compare and measure myself by..."

"...someone else!" shouted Willie, finishing the Captain's words.

"Yes, you are learning the point, Willie," said the Admiral. "Now, Hancock's speech about Daniel's treachery left some settlers not knowing whether they could trust Daniel at all. Therefore, Daniel had to find some way to convince and assure the settlers that he was not a traitor. He decided on a plan to try and win back their trust. Daniel would prove his loyalty to the settlers by leading a raid on a Shawnee village on Paint Creek, and he was able to persuade thirty men to go with him. Daniel also decided that the raid might be helpful in providing more specific information about exactly when the Shawnees were planning to attack Boonesborough."

"Then what happened?" asked Willie, now sitting on the edge of his seat.

"The group left Boonesborough in late August of 1778," the Admiral continued. "However, the day after they left, a third of them decided Daniel was crazy and went back to Boonesborough. The number of men who stayed with Daniel was now only eighteen. They put on war paint and started for the Shawnee Village. One of Daniel's men, Simon Kenton, went ahead of the group as a scout and soon stumbled across two Shawnee warriors. The warriors attacked him, and the rest of their war party joined the fight. Daniel heard the commotion and ran to help. Together, Simon and Daniel gained the upper hand, and the Shawnee warriors fled. The rest of the men caught up with Daniel and Simon, and the group took several of the Shawnees' horses.

"Simon Kenton then went ahead to Paint Creek and discovered that there were no warriors or horses there. He quickly deduced…"

"…that the Shawnee warriors were on their way to attack Boonesborough?" Willie excitedly interrupted the Admiral.

"That's exactly right! Excellent deduction mate," said the Admiral. "You are thinking once again like a true Heroical-Storical-Observicorical-Researchorical-Scientifical-Mate! Here is another Absolutely Genuine Gold Star for you!" The Admiral pulled out from under his sleeve another star and pinned it on Willie's lab coat next to the other three stars.

"I wasn't expecting another Absolutely Genuine Gold Star," said Willie, feeling quite pleased.

"Expectations can be quite a bother," the Captain said. "It's better to lay them aside and allow yourself to be surprised."

"Hmm, I seem to recall having said something very similar earlier," said the Admiral, rubbing his chin. "Moving on," he continued, "Daniel and his men knew they had to get back to Boonesborough quickly and not cross the Shawnees' path on their way. They traveled back by a different route through the forest. They arrived back at Boonesborough on Sunday evening, September 6, 1778, with the grim news that the Shawnees and a militia of British were on their way."

"Then what happened?" asked Tillie.

"The next morning, after Daniel's return," the Admiral continued, "there was still no sign of the Shawnees. The women went to the spring, and the boys watered and fed the live-stock while the men kept a close lookout. Keen-eyed Boone was the first to spot the Shawnees in the distance. There were hundreds of warriors making their way on horseback to Boonesborough."

"And only sixty men to fight off their attack," said Tillie.

"An outstanding recall of an important detail, Tillie!" said the Admiral. "Indeed there were only sixty men at Boonesborough. You are conducting yourself in the very truest tradition of a Heroical-Storical-Observicorical-Researchorical-Scientifical-Mate. An Absolutely Genuine Gold Star for you, mate!" A gold star suddenly appeared in the Admiral's hand. He pinned it on Tillie's lab coat.

"Where were we, mates? Of course, of course," continued the Admiral, "The Shawnee warriors were on the warpath! They rode out of the forest single file into the meadow, prepared for a battle with the settlers. They had first planned to demand surrender, and had even brought extra horses to bring the women back to Fort Detroit in comfort. They were hoping that Boone would keep his promise to surrender Boonesborough to them.

"As Daniel and the settlers stood facing the Shawnees, at a good distance, the interpreter, Pompey, yelled for Daniel Boone. 'Give up, Boone!' Daniel yelled back that the settlers were not going to surrender. Pompey shouted back that Chief Blackfish was there to accept the surrender of Boonesborough and that he expected Boone to keep his word. Pompey continued by saying that he even had letters from the governor, promising that the settlers would be guaranteed a safe trip back to Fort Detroit. The settlers all crowded around Daniel, telling him to yell out to Pompey to see the letters, but then something unexpected happened."

"What?" asked Willie and Tillie, together.

"A very touching moment," said the Captain, as he brought out a handkerchief from his pocket and began to dab his eye. "Daniel Boone heard a familiar voice calling him from the distance, 'Sheltowee, Sheltowee!' It was Chief Blackfish, calling out to his beloved adopted son. The Shawnee Chief had tears running down his cheeks, and Daniel decided to go out of the fort's gate and meet the Chief. They embraced, and the Chief asked Boone, 'My son, what made you run away from me?' Daniel answered, 'Because I wanted to see...'"

"...my wife and children," Tillie interrupted.

The Captain continued, "The Chief told Boone that he would have let him go back to his family if only Boone had asked him."

"Daniel did not answer the Chief, because he knew that might cause more problems," said the Admiral. "Daniel wanted the conversation to begin on another subject, making peace with the Shawnees, so that a battle could be avoided."

"Daniel knew that lives and property were at stake," said the Captain. "In fact, the independence of the new nation called the United States of America was at stake." He stood stiffly at attention, and offered a crisp salute.

The Admiral continued, "Blackfish handed Daniel the letter from Governor Hamilton, and said that he had two choices. Either Daniel could surrender the fort and then he and the settlers would be escorted back to Fort Detroit by the Shawnee and the British militia, or the fort would be destroyed by the Shawnee warriors, along with everyone in it. Chief Blackfish knew that there were many warriors who wanted revenge on the whitemen, no matter the cost.

"Daniel told Blackfish that he would have to discuss it with the other leaders at the fort before a decision could be given. Blackfish agreed and Daniel and the Chief smoked a pipe together."

"Both men respected and cared for each other, and both really wanted peace," said the Captain.

"Daniel came back to the fort and spoke with the other leaders of the settlers," continued the Captain. "Daniel showed them the letter from Governor Hamilton, which said that the settlers would be given safe passage back to Fort Detroit, but they would have to give their loyalty to the British king. Some of the settlers became angry, and swore that they would never surrender to the British."

"What's wrong with the settlers surrendering and giving their loyalty to the British king?" asked Tillie. "At least they would be safe and not lose their lives."

"Good question, mate!" said the Admiral. "They certainly had that choice, but if you realize what the results of that would have been, you will see that it was not a good one. Many of the settlers had left England and come to America to be independent of the laws and rule of Britain. Being under British rule again would be the opposite of everything the settlers wanted. In fact, a number of them, in many areas in North America, would choose to risk their lives rather than be under British control, and you will see that this is exactly what the settlers of Boonesborough did. Write this on your notepads: two years earlier, in July 1776, thirteen formerly British colonies told Britain and her King that they wanted to be independent and rule themselves from now on. The British, of course, wanted to try to stop them, and this resulted in the War of Independence, but that is a Heroical Storical for another time.

"As a man of deep conviction and purpose, Daniel had no intention of betraying the settlers by surrendering to the Shawnees and British, but he did want a peaceful solution to the conflict. He suggested to the men that they try to sign a peace treaty with the Shawnee. Daniel's brother, Squire, did not want to surrender, saying that he 'would never give up, but would fight till death.' They voted, and the settlers decided to fight. Daniel met again with Chief Blackfish later that afternoon, and told him that the leaders needed more time to consider. Chief Blackfish agreed to give them more time."

"I thought Daniel Boone had already made up his mind to fight the Shawnee," said Willie.

"In fact, all the settlers had agreed on it," said the Admiral, "but Daniel knew that if the Chief gave them more time to consider, the settlers could use it to make additional preparations for the battle to come."

The Captain continued, "All that day and the next, the people worked to prepare for a siege. The women went to the spring and bravely filled every bucket and container they could find with water. They needed it for drinking, but they also needed it to put out fires. The Shawnee were known for shooting flaming arrows during battle, and the settlers didn't want the fort to catch on fire. Some of the men also began digging a well inside the compound." The Captain suddenly put a hat on a stick and moved the stick up and down.

"What are you doing?" asked Tillie.

"What I am doing is what the women and children did at Boonesborough!" said the Captain.

"Put hats on sticks?" asked Willie. "Why would anyone do that?"

The Captain replied, "The women marched around back and forth before the gates wearing men's clothes and the children put hats on sticks so that from the outside of the fort it looked like there were more men defending than there actually were. Daniel had told the Shawnee that they had a lot more men at Boonesborough than they really did."

"Why did he tell a lie?" asked Willie.

"He lied to save lives," said the Admiral. "At times, one must choose a greater good, even if it means telling a lie, but let me remind you of this point, mates. As a matter of principle, telling lies is never wise or the right thing to do. Daniel understood this point.

"That evening, Daniel Boone and some other leaders from the fort met with Chief Blackfish again. Daniel told him that the settlers in the fort had decided they would not surrender 'as long as there was a man living.' Now Blackfish was in a tight spot, because he had ordered the Shawnee warriors not to massacre the settlers, but if there was to be a battle, that was probably what would happen. He suggested that the settlers meet with all the Shawnee chiefs and try to draw up a peace treaty. Boone agreed and they planned to start the following day.

"As part of the negotiations, the Shawnee would be allowed to use the settlers' livestock and crops, and the women and children would be able to peacefully come in or leave the fort. To start the peace talks, the women made a delicious meal for the Shawnee, not only as a welcome, but also to convince them that there were plenty of supplies in the fort to withstand a prolonged siege. Daniel kept trying to keep the peace talks going because he wanted more men from Virginia to arrive to help fight if the peace treaty was broken."

"What did they eat?" asked Tillie.

"I'll answer that one," said the Captain, as he began to nibble on a corncob. "The women prepared a tasty meal consisting of buffalo tongue, venison, cheese, milk, bread and garden vegetables including corn on the cob," said the Captain as he took a big bite from the cob.

"Buffalo tongue?" asked Willie.

"Buffalo tongue?" asked Tillie.

"Buffalo tongue, indeed," said the Captain, "and it is quite tasty, roasted." He suddenly brought out a buffalo tongue.

Willie and Tillie both looked at each other, feeling sick and almost the same color green as Captain Perry's feathers.

"Shall we put the buffalo tongue aside, for now?" said the Admiral. "We have more to discover about the battle of Boonesborough. I regret I must also mention that a corn kernel has managed to rest itself on top of your beak, Captain!"

"Thanks, Admiral," said the Captain, as he quickly plucked off the corn kernel. "A true friend will always tell you if you have a corn kernel on your beak."

"Now that we have dealt with corn kernels and buffalo tongues, shall we go back to the Heroical Storical?" asked the Admiral. "I believe we were talking about the peace treaty between the Shawnee and the settlers. It appeared fair to both sides, but Daniel was not convinced it would last. Daniel felt he could not trust the Shawnee because the British were with them and he did not like the part where the settlers would have to swear allegiance to the British king to avoid harm. Blackfish was hopeful that the peace treaty would bring a lasting peace, so he decided that the men from his group should shake hands with Daniel in agreeing to the terms of the peace treaty."

"How long did the peace treaty last?" asked Willie.

"About sixty seconds," said Captain Perry as he looked at a stopwatch.

"Sixty seconds?" asked Tillie.

"Indeed, the long and lasting peace treaty lasted less than one minute," said the Admiral. "After a speech by Chief Blackfish, the frontier leaders met the Shawnee on the field for the handshake. Each of the nine frontier leaders shook hands with the Chiefs, but the hand shaking immediately became an arm wrestling match.

"There were many among the settlers who still did not trust the Shawnee and there were many Shawnee who did not trust the whitemen. When the Shawnees began the handshake, which was more like an embrace, one of the settlers, Richard Callaway, jerked away out of fear and distrust. Richard was known to be hotheaded and mean, and he was the one who appears to have first started scuffling with the Shawnee warriors. Many of the Shawnee reacted by grappling with the settlers, too, and from the fort it must have looked like a real brawl. Suddenly a shot rang out from the fort and the Battle of Boonesborough had finally begun."

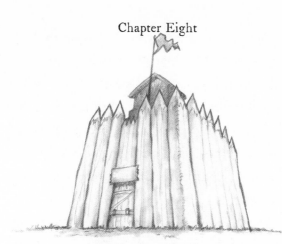

Chapter Eight

The Battle of Boonesborough

The Admiral continued. "The whole area erupted in gunfire, as Shawnees and settlers thought that the other side had set a trap,"

"Everything went crazy!" said the Captain. "More shots were fired from both sides. The Shawnees were hiding behind trees and rocks, shooting at Daniel and the frontier leaders, who were being grabbed by the Shawnees.

Shawnees who were stationed across the river began firing into the fort. Marksmen stationed in the fort fired on the Shawnees in the field. A warrior near Daniel who had been carrying the peace pipe to each leader swung at Daniel with it, slashing him in the back!"

"Ouch! That pipe wasn't very peaceful," said Willie.

"Daniel was slightly hurt," said the Admiral, "but he was alive and very determined to do everything he could to defend the fort and survive the attack. He and the other leaders managed to break free of the Shawnee and began to run back to the fort. An amazing miracle it was that all nine leaders from the fort managed to make it back to the fort alive, but not without some being hit. Daniel's brother, Squire, took a bullet in the shoulder, which knocked him down, but he got up again and made it inside the gate. Once Daniel was back in the fort, he removed the bullet from his brother's shoulder, who had to go to bed for a day to recover. In case a Shawnee broke in, Squire kept an ax by his bed."

"A bullet later hit Daniel's daughter, Jemima, in the backside," said the Captain.

"Talk about a pain in the behind," laughed Willie.

Tillie looked at her brother with disgust, while Captain Perry stifled a chuckle, and his face turned red again. The Admiral was not that amused.

"War is never funny," said Admiral Wright, solemnly. "People give in to their anger and hurt each other, for sometimes the most foolish reasons. If more people learned to share instead of being selfish, there would be no fights over land, and if folks learned how to be kind to each other and respect each other, there would be no more wars over beliefs. Innocent individuals die because they stand up for what they believe is right, such as the right to live without oppression, or to have enough food to eat."

They were all quiet for a moment.

The Admiral suddenly pulled out from the trunk a very old petticoat.

"Why do you have that?" asked Tillie.

"This is a very important collectible from the Battle at Boonesborough," answered the Admiral. "This is the petticoat that Jemima wore when the bullet entered her backside. You see, mates, her very heavy petticoat saved Jemima from serious injury. The bullet hit her in the rump, and it was only partly buried in her skin because the thick fabric of her petticoat acted as a shield and protected her. When Jemima pulled on the cloth, the bullet popped out."

"Like a cork out of a bottle!" said the Captain.

"Truly, but now let us return to the battle," said the Admiral. "The Battle of Boonesborough was well under way, and

Daniel Boone and the rest of the frontier leaders were running for their lives back to the fort." The Admiral pointed to Daniel Boone's hat, which he was still wearing. "This hat, mates, if you recall from my earlier discussion, is the very hat that Daniel Boone wore while dodging Shawnee bullets."

"I understand," said Willie. "Daniel Boone was shot during his run back to the fort. Somebody up there watched out for Daniel when that Shawnee bullet missed his head and only pierced his hat! What an amazing collectible you found, Admiral!"

"Yes, it is, mate, an amazing and rare collectible," said the Admiral.

"Can I wear it?" asked Willie.

"Of course," said the Admiral, as he carefully placed the hat on Willie's head.

"Daniel's hat is way too big for you, it's almost covering your eyes!" laughed Tillie.

"I don't care," said Willie, as he pushed it

further back on his head. "I like it because Daniel Boone wore it and that's enough for me."

"That first day and the next were the worst of the battle," the Admiral continued. "The women cried and screamed. They expected that at any moment the fort would be stormed by hundreds of Shawnee warriors. Cattle and sheep ran everywhere, kicking up clouds of dust, making a black cloud, which when mixed with the gun smoke and fire from the rooftops made it almost impossible to see. That was Thursday. On Friday, Daniel ordered the men to shoot carefully, for they had to save ammunition. The Shawnees also slackened their attack, and as it became quieter, the men heard sounds of digging. Daniel looked over at the Kentucky River. It appeared clear upstream but downstream the current was muddy. What do you think that meant?"

"I know," said Willie. "The Shawnees were digging a tunnel, and the dirt from their shoveling was going into the river."

"Excellent deduction, mate!" the Admiral said, as he gave Willie an enthusiastic slap on the shoulder. "You are indeed continuing to think like a true Heroical-Storical-Observicorical-Researchorical-Scientifical-Mate! Another Absolutely Genuine Gold Star for you!"

The Admiral quickly pinned another star on Willie's lab coat and continued. "Daniel did discover that the Shawnees were digging a tunnel from the riverbank toward the settlement. The Shawnees were attempting to use fancy siege techniques under the guidance of the French-Canadian military leader De Quindre."

"That's right," said the Captain. "The Shawnees, with De Quindre's direction, were trying to shovel under an outer wall of the settlement and make it collapse. If the tunnel didn't work, a powder charge would be exploded. This would definitely make the wall collapse and cause major damage. With the walls of Boonesborough down, the Shawnee warriors, with some of the British at their side, could rush in and seize control."

"Precisely spoken, Captain," said the Admiral.

"Sneak attack, how scary," said Willie.

"It was a bit fearful," said the Admiral, "but Daniel faced fear and courageously fought on. He came up with a plan for the settlers to start digging their own tunnel, as a countermine. He began to dig a four-foot-deep passage that would run under the cabins, exactly parallel to the settlement's river wall. Daniel hoped that the settler's tunnel would cross the Shawnee tunnel so he could launch a surprise counterattack."

"Digging a tunnel was hot and very tiring work," said Captain Perry. "Settlers became cranky and irritable because food and water, not to mention ammunition, became scarce as the siege lasted another week. Thirsty cattle in the fort lowed miserably. Everyone was exhausted from having little sleep. The settlers knew that only a thin wall of spikes, the feeble wooden palisade, separated them from death."

"The Captain is correct in describing the scene inside the fort as very discouraging," said the Admiral, "but soon it got much worse. Friday night, the Shawnees intensified their gunfire, which was to cover their efforts to set fire to the settlement. They would run up in twos and threes, carrying torches to throw into the fort. Amidst the confusion, Daniel kept a clear head and acted decisively in organizing a group of settlers to put out the roof fires with the buckets of water that the women and children had worked hard to collect. They were aided by Squire Boone's new invention. In addition to using water buckets to douse the fires, Squire devised the first known squirt gun to extinguish the flames that were better put out with a long stream of water, strategically shot."

"Brilliant idea," said Willie.

"Absolutely," said the Captain, who reached into the trunk and brought out an old rifle barrel. The Captain pulled the trigger and a forceful stream of water suddenly squirted from the rifle barrel and hit Willie in the face.

The powerful squirt knocked Daniel Boone's hat right off Willie's head. "Wow," said Willie after sputtering and gasping in surprise. "I want one, too!" he exclaimed as he wiped off his face with his hand.

"You might," said the Captain, "get one, mate, but don't hold those hopes too high. Rifle-barreled squirt guns are hard to find. Now that I think of it, this might be useful to write down, so get your pens and pads out. Here's a famous fact for you: Squire's rifled-barreled squirt gun was the very first squirt gun ever invented. If you notice, 'Squire' sounds a lot like 'squirt.' It was best at extinguishing most of the very difficult fires, like those in the far corners of the rooftops. And now, because of this fact, I have a most profound conclusion to speak about."

"What's that?" the twins asked.

"I have concluded," the Captain paused to declare in a very firm voice, "that the Battle of Boonesborough was won by the power of a squirt gun; and this conclusion was arrived at by rigorous study and careful analysis. This process is known as research!"

Willie's stomach turned a bit when he heard that word.

The Admiral suddenly cleared his throat and appeared significantly bothered about the Captain's conclusion. He frowned a bit and said, "I beg your pardon but I must interject here, if you would be so kind as to give me a moment. Ah, I hope you forgive me, but I must speak my mind on the matter. Well, frankly, I feel that perhaps your conclusion may lack a certain, ah, academic quality."

The Admiral became increasingly exasperated. He sputtered a bit, twitching his mustache. Finally, he said, "Well, your statement is quite absurd. Squirt guns do not win battles. Squirt guns may help, but they are highly unlikely to be the only factor responsible for winning a battle."

The Admiral turned slightly to Willie and Tillie. "I shall have to ask you to bear my repetition on the point, mates," he said, and then, turning back to the Captain, "but it is only truly fair to say and conclude that the squirt gun that Squire invented played only a part in the settlers' final victory. Furthermore, it is a most far-fetched and erroneous conclusion that the Battle of Boonesborough was won by the power of a squirt gun alone. As faithful historians and observers, Captain, we must be extremely careful about the statements we make to these budding Heroical-Storical-Observicorical-Researchorical-Scientific-Mates."

"Point well taken, Admiral," said the Captain, humbly, "and I do not differ with any word that you have spoken. It was my error; I can be a bit absentminded at times. I simply forgot one small six-letter word."

"What word was that?" asked Tillie.

"Almost!" said the Captain.

"Almost?" asked Willie.

"Exactly," said the Captain. "What I meant to say was that the Battle of Boonesborough was almost won by the power of a squirt gun. Almost brings a completely different meaning to the sentence." The Captain began to eat another cracker.

"Yes, yes, very true," said the Admiral. "Do forgive me for my outburst. I am very passionate about truth!"

"I understand completely, Admiral," said the Captain.

"Very well, mates," said the Admiral. "Shall we move on?"

"I'm ready," said Tillie.

"What happened after the squirt gun action?" asked Willie.

The Admiral lowered his voice and leaned forward. "The siege continued for another week, digging and gunfire during the day, and gunfire and flying torches at night. There were insults and bullets exchanged, and casualties on both sides. On the eleventh night, the battle intensified again. The flashes from the guns of both sides lit the sky like fireworks. The fires from the torches thrown by the Shawnees were spreading faster than the settlers could put them out. The battle grew worse, the Shawnees' tunnel was coming closer and the settlers were outnumbered. It appeared that the best efforts of Daniel and the settlers to keep Boonesborough from falling into Shawnee and British control would soon be over."

"I will mention for the Admiral's benefit

that the power of Squire's rifle-barreled squirt gun was not enough to win the battle," the Captain interrupted.

"Good, Captain, thinking soundly now," said the Admiral, as he gave him a pat on the head. "Daniel was shot in the upper shoulder as he bolted across the yard in a blaze of gunfire from the Shawnees. The news of the injury spread and the Shawnees were declaring victory and began yelling, 'We've killed Boone! We've killed Boone!'"

"How hopeless! Everything's going wrong. What's going to happen now?" asked Willie.

"Plenty is going to happen," said the Admiral, opening his eyes very wide, "but now,"—he lowered his voice and got very close to the twins—"you shall see the happenings beyond what you have ever thought or imagined."

Chapter Nine

The Extraordinary
Black-Rimmed Glasses

Willie asked with a strange tingle of excitement. "What do you mean when you say that I will see beyond what I have ever thought or imagined?"

"You'll know what I mean in just a little while," said the Admiral. "Carry on, Captain, with the Heroical Storical."

"I would be delighted to continue," said the Captain. "Where did we leave off? Oh yes, now I recall, Daniel had been shot and the settlers were in hopeless circumstances with the fort on fire and the Shawnees digging their way in through an underground tunnel."

"I would have given up," said Tillie.

"Daniel Boone never, never, never, never gave up hope," continued the Captain.

"Why?" asked Willie.

"Faith Power," said the Captain, as he puffed out his chest and looked up. "Faith Power powers up in the face of fear and impossibility. Faith Power gave Daniel plenty of courage, strength and wisdom, and opened up the possibility for Divine Intervention. Daniel needed lots of Faith Power because he had been shot, Boonesborough was going up in flames and a Shawnee tunnel was about to break through and collapse the outer wall."

"Well, what happened?" asked Tillie.

"Something very unusual," said the Admiral, "and that something was something that Boone had no control over, nor did the

Shawnee warriors."

"Too many somethings," said the Captain.

"What something was that?" asked Willie.

The Admiral suddenly stood up and announced, "The time has come for something to happen." He paused for a moment.

"For what?" asked Tillie.

"To put on your Extraordinary Black-Rimmed Glasses," declared the Admiral in a very solemn voice.

Before an eye could blink or a finger snap, the Admiral's countenance suddenly changed. There appeared on his face Extraordinary Black-Rimmed Glasses that were dotted with white polka dots that sparkled in the light.

"Wow," said Willie, "I've never seen so many sparkly dots on glasses before."

"However extraordinary I look," said the Admiral, "it is nothing compared to what we are about to see and experience. Put on your Extraordinary Black-Rimmed Glasses now, mates!"

Willie and Tillie reached into their very yellow plastic pocket protectors and carefully put their Extraordinary Black-Rimmed Glasses on.

"What about the Captain?" asked Tillie. "Doesn't he need Extraordinary Black-Rimmed Glasses?"

"Never mind me," said the Captain. He spun around and faced Willie and Tillie, wearing the same Extraordinary Black-Rimmed Glasses, which were dotted with white polka dots that sparkled in the light, exactly like the Admiral's glasses.

"I want sparkly white polka dots on my glasses, too," whined Tillie.

"For now, the sparkly white polka dots are reserved exclusively for the Captain and me," said the Admiral. "They are only a distinguishing factor and have no functional purpose. Remember, mates, the power of the glasses is in the lens, not the frame."

"I don't see anything extraordinary through my black-rimmed glasses," said Tillie, who was feeling a bit cranky because she wanted sparkly white polka dots on her glasses, too! However, she couldn't stay cranky for long because in the next moment Tillie was standing in a dark, cool forest, facing a burning fort.

"You are right here in the Heroical Storical Laboratory under my Ship Shop," said the Admiral. "Remember, these glasses are extraordinary. They enlarge your vision so you can see in a way that you have never known before. The power of these Extraordinary Black-Rimmed Glasses enables us to see beyond what is present and into a window of the past. We can also experience the moments in the past, as if we were right there. You may think you are there because you will experience everything as if you really are there, but in actuality here is where you really are. As to how I am able to accomplish this, there are mysteries that few will ever know, and this is one of them!"

The Captain interrupted, "Extraordinary Black-Rimmed Glasses will make us able to discover and learn from an eyewitness view all about the final moments of Daniel Boone's heroic stand during the Battle of Boonesborough."

"How can we see what's going on inside the fort from here in the forest?" asked Tillie.

"Follow me," said the Captain, flying off toward the fort.

"Perhaps I may assist a bit as well," said the Admiral with a chuckle. A mysterious gust of wind blew around the three of them and carried them up to a cabin rooftop inside the settlement at Boonesborough.

They stood looking down at the settlement and the forest beyond, from the rooftop of one of the few cabins that were not burning.

"This is fantastic, I can see everything!" said Willie. "The settlers are using Squire's squirt guns to put out the roof fires."

"I know," said Tillie, "but they're losing the battle!" She was very concerned. "There's no way they'll be able to put out all those fires with those squirt guns and buckets of water."

"You are correct, Tillie," said the Admiral. "Daniel needs help! It's time for Divine Intervention!"

"Divine Intervention?" asked Willie and Tillie.

"Divine Intervention, exactly!" said the Admiral.

"You said that before," said Willie. "What do you mean?"

"What he means," said the Captain, fluttering and landing on the Admiral's shoulder, "is that Daniel needs help from a power bigger than himself."

Before the Captain finished his words, lightning flashed and thunder boomed.

"Wow!" said Willie and Tillie.

"Divine intervention," said the Admiral.

"That is precisely what Daniel needs," said the Captain, and began to eat another cracker.

"I felt a raindrop," said Tillie.

"Me too," said Willie.

"You mates will need these," said the Admiral, as he handed umbrellas to Willie and Tillie. "Soon you shall be feeling much more than a drop or two."

The Admiral opened his swirling rainbow umbrella over himself and the Captain. The colors were dimmer now, and not gleaming much at all.

The rain began to pour down, and it poured for a long time. The group sat under their umbrellas, watching the rain fall and hearing the hissing sound of fires sputtering out.

"The rain is putting out all the fires," said Willie.

"The men are acting crazy," said Tillie. "They're jumping up and down and they don't care that their clothes are getting soaked."

"Daniel and the settlers are rejoicing that the rain is putting out the fires. Of course, the battle is not over yet," said the Admiral. "You see, the Shawnee have not given up their plan to tunnel into Boonesborough. Look at all the mud that is going into the river from their shovels. The tunnel could reach the wall at any moment."

"I hear something. It sounds like scraping," said Willie.

"What you are hearing is the sound of shovels that are digging closer and closer to the compound," said the Admiral.

"I'm scared," said Tillie.

"That's how most of the women and children are feeling right now," said the Captain. "They are praying and huddled into the corners of their cabins under blankets."

"What's going to happen?" asked Willie.

"Nothing, for now," said the Admiral.

"Nothing?" asked Willie.

"Yes, nothing. Watch and wait," said the Admiral.

The group sat quietly on the rooftop waiting for nothing to happen. After what seemed like a long time, the rain began to lessen, and Willie and Tillie noticed that the fires had died out and that the Shawnee camp had been disbanded.

"I don't hear scraping sounds anymore," said Willie.

"An exact observation, mate!" said the Admiral.

"I think I know what happened," said Tillie, quietly. "The Shawnees' tunnel has..."

"...completely collapsed because of the rain," shouted Willie.

"I was about to say just that," said Tillie.

"Mates, no quarreling on the rooftop," said the Admiral. "You are both brilliant and becoming more and more like true Heroical-Storical-Observicorical-Researchorical-Scientifical-Mates. I hereby grant you each another Absolutely Genuine Gold Star!" The Admiral brought out two stars and pinned them next to the others, right above the lab coat pockets of Willie and Tillie.

"Willie still has one more Absolutely Genuine Gold Star than me," said Tillie.

"Tillie, dear, once again, you have done your math correctly," said the Admiral. "Remember, knowledge and understanding are more valuable than gold. You are both correct that the rain has collapsed the Shawnee's tunnel. The rain has certainly daunted the warriors' efforts to destroy Boonesborough."

"Look, mates," said the Captain, pointing to a clearing in the woods.

They could see an angry man, stomping his feet and shaking his fist.

"It is the French leader, De Quindre, who came up with the idea of digging the tunnel," said the Admiral. "He certainly appears to be hopping mad, a most undesirable state for anyone to be in. As you may notice, the Shawnees are not acting like De Quindre. They are mounting their horses and beginning to ride away. They had fought long and hard, but it was not enough to defeat Daniel Boone and Divine Intervention."

"Why didn't Divine Intervention work for the Shawnees?" asked Willie.

"One never knows how the forces beyond our understanding move or whence they come and go," said the Admiral, somewhat solemnly.

"A miracle indeed," said the Captain, "and now it's time to celebrate! The Battle of Boonesborough is over, and all the weary settlers and Shawnee warriors can get some rest and food."

The Admiral folded up his umbrella, which didn't seem to be wet at all! The Captain fluttered off the Admiral's shoulder and suddenly appeared with an oversized brass horn. He took a deep breath and blew it until he went almost purple in the face. Then he started to put the horn down, and was so dizzy, he almost fell off the roof! Willie caught him just in time.

"Can I try the horn?" asked Willie.

"Not yet, mate," said the Captain, as he steadied himself on the roof. "Look, in the center of the fort, there's a man running in circles shouting something."

Willie looked down at the fort and saw a burly bearded man with a torn shirt, running in circles shouting, "It's collapsed! It's collapsed; our prayers are answered! The Shawnees have left, they've left, they've left!"

"Look at all the women and children coming out of their cabins," said Tillie. "They're weeping for joy! They're glad the battle is over."

"Yes, they are," said the Admiral. "After twelve days of grueling attack, the Battle of Boonesborough is finally over, and Daniel Boone has led the small group of settlers to victory with great amounts of courage, perseverance, Faith Power and, of course, a bit of Divine Intervention."

Willie and Tillie continued to watch the settlers coming out of their cabins and greeting each other.

"Do you have any binoculars, Admiral?" asked Willie. "I'd like to look closer at the faces of the settlers."

"Certainly," said the Admiral. "I do happen to have some very green binoculars." He quickly revealed four pairs of very green binoculars.

"I remember seeing these in the glass case back at the Admiral's Ship Shop," said Willie.

The Admiral handed them out.

Together, and at the exact same time, the Merriweather Mates put the very green binoculars up to their Extraordinary Black-Rimmed Glasses. "I think I see Daniel Boone again," said Willie.

"How do you know?" asked Tillie.

"He's got a torn shirt and a bandage on his shoulder. I remember Daniel was shot there," said Willie. He was silent for a moment. Then he began to grin. "That's weird."

"What?" asked Tillie.

"He's rolling in the mud and laughing," said Willie.

"That's a-right mate, it's Daniel in the mud," said the Captain. "He's overjoyed that the Battle is over!"

"Daniel took account of the losses afterwards," said the Admiral. "He was quite thankful that only two settlers had died, and only four others were wounded, but there were further costs to pay. Thirty-seven Shawnees had lost their lives in the conflict. The crops and most of the livestock had also been destroyed. War is costly. The Battle of Boonesborough had been the longest siege in the history of Kentucky!"

"Can you guess how many pounds of lead were shot at the settlers?" asked the Captain.

"Fifty pounds," said Tillie.

"Seventy-five pounds," said Willie.

"You're both wrong, but if you add your pounds together you'll get the correct answer," said the Captain.

"Oh, that's one hundred and thirty-five," said Willie confidently.

"No, Willie, seventy-five plus fifty is one hundred and twenty-five. My math is always correct," said Tillie, with a flip of her ponytail.

"Tillie is correct," said the Admiral. "Nearly one hundred twenty-five pounds of lead had been shot at the settlers."

"That's a big bunch of bullets!" said the Captain.

"This was later picked out of cabin walls and the wooden fence surrounding the settlement and melted in molds to make new bullets," the Admiral finished.

"What happened to the British after the battle?" said Willie.

"Excellent question, mate," said the Admiral. "I was about to tell you. Look carefully at all those settlers rejoicing. You can see now that Daniel is out of the mud, washed off a bit, and standing next to one of the burnt cabins looking at all the damage. Little does Daniel know that at this very time General George Rogers Clark is marching his troops to capture British-held forts at Cahokia, Kaskaskia and Vincennes in the area we now know as Illinois and Indiana. Clark will continue his campaign and successfully attack and capture Fort Detroit, where Governor Hamilton will be a prisoner. The Battle of Boonesborough was a great event in history for several reasons. It kept the settlers in control of the land that they made their home. It proved not only that they could withstand the attack of the Shawnee backed by the British, but also it was one of many struggles to prove that the new Americans could keep their independence from

Britain by defending their right to freedom."

"That's why the Battle of Boonesborough is important!" said Willie.

"What would have happened if Boonesborough had fallen into British hands?" asked Tillie.

"I will tell you," said the Admiral.

"There would have been a lot more tea and crumpets," said Willie.

"Possibly," said the Admiral, "but Tillie has another excellent question that needs an answer. I was just about to..."

"I'd like to answer it, if you don't mind," interrupted the Captain.

"Go ahead," said the Admiral, with a chuckle, "but no absurd reasoning and concluding."

The Captain flew up to the Admiral's shoulder. "If Boonesborough had fallen into British hands, then all Kentucky settlements would have too, and it's possible that the Americans would have lost the war with

Britain. General Clark's supply lines and only exit would have been cut, because Boonesborough was the center of the frontier pathway to new settlements in the West. Clark would have had to end his campaign to secure that area, which, if you remember the map, stretched from the Appalachian Mountains to the Mississippi.

"Winning the Battle of Boonesborough was a test and Daniel Boone and the settlers passed. The small settlement survived, and that meant that Kentucky and the Ohio River Valley wilderness could remain free and independent as part of the new nation that would call itself the United States of America."

"That's amazing," said Tillie.

"Excellent explanation, Captain!" the Admiral beamed.

"America would have had less America, if Daniel Boone lost," said Willie.

"That's rrrrrright!" shouted the Captain.

"Kentucky, Illinois and Indiana would have likely ended up being ruled by Britain, and a lot more tea parties would have been going on."

The Admiral brought out his Quantum Space Atomic Clock. "Speaking of tea, mates, soon it will be time for another sip of my peppermint tea back at the Ship Shop, and time, too, for my very furry slippers! With all this rain, my toes are a bit on the chilly side. We must go back! Back to the Heroical Storical Laboratory...

in the Ship Shop at Merriweather Bay,

on Nantucket Island,

in the country called America,

on the planet Earth that resides

in the solar system

of our most glorious sun!"

"I thought we never left the Heroical Storical Laboratory," said Tillie.

"That's a mystery," said the Captain, with a twinkle in his eye.

"I don't want to leave yet," said Willie. "I haven't met Daniel Boone."

"Hmm," said the Admiral, stroking his mustache. "I suppose that can be arranged, before our journey back," he said with a gleam in his eye.

The Captain stroked his beard, thoughtfully, with a quick glance at the Admiral. Suddenly there was a strong gust of wind, and the group was carried down from the cabin roof to the center of Boonesborough. Willie and Tillie now stood next to the large mud puddle that Daniel had been rolling in.

"There he is, it's Daniel Boone! I know it's him," said Willie quite excitedly. "He's talking to his brother, Squire. Can he hear me? Can I talk to him?"

"Certainly," said the Admiral.

Willie slowly approached Daniel Boone and pulled on his tattered leather coat to get his attention. "Excuse me, Mr. Boone, but I have been watching you and I think you're a hero! A Character Champion—and someone I want to be just like when I grow up."

"A hero! A Character Champion? A mighty fine compliment. Thank you!" said Mr. Boone. "What can I do for you?"

"Uh, can I shake your hand?" Willie asked.

Daniel Boone reached out his hand and Willie shook it for what seemed like the longest time.

"I think we ought to give this fine lad something," said Squire Boone. He reached behind him, pulled out a rifle-barreled squirt gun and gave it to Willie.

"Thank you, Daniel Boone and Squire!" Willie gushed. "Thank you, thank you so much, this is going to go into my treasure of collectibles, and I will never lose it!"

A loud beeping noise suddenly filled the air. The Admiral looked at his Quantum Space Atomic Clock. "Willie," he said, "we must return now, or it will be too late."

"Too late for what?" asked Tillie. "I thought all we had to do to return to the Heroical Storical Laboratory was to take our glasses off."

"That is essentially correct, but there is always more to everything than you can know, imagine or think," said the Admiral.

The beeping noise grew louder. "Mates, there is no time to waste," said the Admiral in a commanding tone. "On the count of four, grab hands, or a wing tip, and jump! Captain, before I forget, you must place in your beak Willie's rifle-barreled squirt gun, a very valuable collectible, indeed."

The Captain quickly put the squirt gun in his beak, and in the next moment the Merriweather Mates shouted:

"One, two, three, four, JUMP!"

And jump they did, with all the might they could muster. The mates flew in the air and, within the blink of an eye, they were back in the Heroical Storical Laboratory and standing square in the center of the Admiral's rug of the solar system.

"My Extraordinary Black-Rimmed Glasses have disappeared," said Willie.

"Mine too," said Tillie, who had developed a new liking for them.

"Where did they go?" asked Willie.

"They no longer exist here, for us," the

Admiral replied. "Their purpose has been served, but perhaps they will return." The Captain and he shared a glance.

"Where's my squirt gun?" asked Willie, while looking around the room.

"Don't fret, mate," said the Captain, as he handed the squirt gun to Willie.

"Thanks. I've had the most fun I've ever had and I have definitely brought the best part home with me."

"And what's the best part?" asked Tillie.

"My rifle-barreled squirt gun!" said Willie.

Tillie rolled her eyes and said, "You'll never change. All you ever think about is your junk that you call collectibles." She paused for a moment. "Well, a rifle-barreled squirt gun may not be your usual junk, but you simply have got to start caring more about learning."

"I've learned how to be a true Heroical-Storical-Observicorical-Researchorical-Scientifical-Mate, haven't I? Just look at how many Absolutely Genuine Gold Stars I have," said Willie. "In fact, I have a total of six, one more than...."

Before Willie could finish his sentence, a deafening boom broke the air. The mates covered their ears.

"Ouch, that was loud!" said Tillie.

"What was it?" asked Willie.

"Perhaps it was a sonic boom," said the Admiral quite calmly, as if to indicate that deafening booms are a common occurrence. He carefully reached into his pocket and pulled out his white gloves, which he began to put on. "Now the Captain and I must return, another journey is to be made. The Shiny Shiny Silver Ship awaits us; and a new exciting Heroical Storical is in the making, and of course, discovery and adventure are calling."

"Can we go?" asked the twins.

"Not this time mates, better to scurry your feet home," the Admiral replied. "I believe Miss

Chatterberry will be concerned. After all, Tillie, if I'm not mistaken, you neglected to call and tell her that you and Willie would be late!"

Admiral Wright became silent and still. He then took a deep breath and began a solemn speech:

"The Captain and I must bid you farewell, for now, but remember, mates: The memories of our adventure, our learning and discovery, will always be with you, and of course, the indomitable spirit of Daniel Boone will inspire and encourage you to be a Character Champion for today and tomorrow. You have gained new skills of thinking and observing, and these will also stay with you. However, you must always practice, practice and practice (the Admiral's voice became louder with each word) to become increasingly more like a true Heroical-Storical-Observicorical-Researchorical-Scientifical-Mates. If not, your skills will become weak and useless. You must use them, or lose them! Moreover, remember the words of a very wise character, 'Life is not only a race, but a journey where one learns to walk in wisdom, by avoiding what's wrong and doing what's right, serving others, like the truest of true Character Champions always do!' Never forget that yesterday is history, tomorrow is a mystery, and today is a gift. That is why some call it 'the present!'"

"And mates," said the Captain, "Write this on the doorpost of your home: Character is not something you ask for. You have to earn it, like respect. You have to develop it, like strength. Daniel Boone had it. He didn't take the easy way; he took the right way and cared about others and served them. He never gave up. Now that's a real Character Champion!"

"Thank you, Captain, for those good words." The Admiral paused, then straightened up and lifted his hand, gave a stiff, dignified salute and boldly declared, "My friends, the

Captain and I are now onward and upward!"

The Admiral opened his swirling rainbow umbrella, and lifted it overhead. As Willie and Tillie watched, the colors began swirling faster and faster, growing in brightness until the Admiral and Captain were surrounded by crystalline sparkling, swirling rainbow light, its radiance lit the room, like the morning light breaking through the dawn.

To the most wonderful surprise of Willie and Tillie, sparkles and shimmery rainbow glitters sprinkled their faces and, to add to their further delight, silvery swirling patterns of diamonds, triangles, and circles shone on everything in the room. They continued to watch as the rainbow light surrounding the Admiral and Captain grew to a brightness of brilliant white which appeared to almost be the shiniest silver imaginable, (just like the Shiny Shiny Silver Ship) and then, in the brightest flash of light, they vanished, leaving behind a twinkly flurry of sparkly silver sprinkles.

"Where did they go?" screamed Tillie.

"Let's climb the stairs and see if we can see them from the rooftop!" yelled Willie.

Willie and Tillie raced up the long winding stairs with a speed they had never known—one hundred twenty-three stairs might as well have been only three.

Willie and Tillie opened the rooftop door and saw the Shiny Shiny Silver Ship flying into the clouds. The Admiral and Captain leaned over the rail to wave good-bye.

Willie waved back and something fell out of his pocket.

Tillie looked down and saw the compass.

"You never returned the Admiral's compass!" yelled Tillie.

"Oh no," moaned Willie. He suddenly shouted the loudest he ever had, "I have your compass! Your spinning compass!"

The Admiral heard, but he didn't mind.

Chapter Ten

The Next Day
at School

Willie Venturely woke up very early the following morning and for the first time in a long, long time, he wanted to go to school. Not only did Willie want to go to school, he also was determined to go to the library. In fact, he couldn't wait to get there to do the research for his report on Daniel Boone, the frontiersman whose hand he had shaken and the frontiersman whose battles with the Shawnees he had witnessed. Willie got to the library before school began. Mrs. Dexter, the librarian, almost fell over as Willie rushed past her into the biography section. Then she almost fainted from shock as she watched Willie check out every book on Daniel Boone. He quickly skimmed the books. He knew what he was going to write. He reached into his backpack and pulled out his notebook paper and pencil, and began. This time Willie didn't struggle with Mind Wander, nor was he tempted to copy out of books. Willie wrote and wrote and wrote all about the Battle of Boonesborough, Boone's kidnapping, Chief Blackfish, the grueling gauntlet, the not-so-peaceful peace treaty, the Shawnees' tunnel, the burning cabins, the rainstorm, Divine Intervention and Squire's rifle-barreled squirt gun. Willie had never written so fast. It was amazing and almost supernatural that Willie was completely done with his Boone report in less than one hour. That was a good thing, because the first bell had rung and it was time for Miss Dullywinkle's class to begin.

Tillie passed Willie while on her way to the classroom and, of course, couldn't resist saying, "Is your Daniel Boone report done? It's due today."

Willie smiled and said nothing.

Willie and Tillie took their seats. Miss Dullywinkle called roll and announced, "All Daniel Boone reports are due now. Please bring them up to the front of the class."

Willie reached into his notebook and began to tear out the sheets of paper that he had been writing on that morning in the library. He counted aloud the number of pages as he ripped out one after another. One, two, three, four, five, six, seven, eight, nine, ten, eleven ....all the way up to twenty-one pages.

Willie had never written that much in his whole life and not one word of it was copied from a book. He actually needed a stapler! He stood up, carrying his twenty-one pages, and went over to Miss Dullywinkle's desk and stapled them together. Willie felt quite accomplished because he had written something he was proud of for the first time ever.

After lunch, Miss Dullywinkle made an unusual announcement: "Class, I have read over your reports and there is one that is outstanding."

Tillie looked at her brother and smiled. She couldn't wait to hear her name called out.

Miss Dullywinkle continued. "Until today, I have never heard of the concept of a 'Heroical Storical' as defined by the student whose paper I am holding. However, even I can learn and grow! This student defines a Heroical Storical as an extremely intriguing story in a hero's life and tells a very well written and captivating story himself. I would like Willie Venturely to come to the front of the room, please."

Tillie gasped.

"Would you please read your 'Heroical Storical' about Daniel Boone and the Battle of

Boonesborough aloud to the class?" Miss Dullywinkle asked.

The other students murmured, "Willie? What's he got to say?"

Willie stood up, walked to the front of the class and sat on the stool. This time he was not going to be wearing the dunce cap!

Willie began to read.

And he couldn't stop; he read aloud his Heroical Storical, but he added a lot more detail that he hadn't even written in his paper. Were the students desk fishing or falling asleep; or was mean Billy Bones shooting a nasty spitball? Absolutely not. The students had never heard Daniel Boone or any other historical hero talked about in this way before and they wanted to hear more. Willie even brought out his rifle-barreled squirt gun. Everyone wanted to see it squirt. Willie carefully filled it with water; and he honestly didn't know how it happened, but in the very next moment, the squirt gun launched a gush of water that squirted Tillie right in the face. All the students became very quiet. Some were a bit worried about how Tillie might respond; after all, she was the reigning queen of research-report writing, and now she had been dethroned by her brother and, to make the matter worse, she had just been humiliated in front of her classmates by a big squirt of water in the face. Nothing happened for the first minute. The room was strangely quiet; even a pin drop could be heard. But out of that strange quietness came a soft giggle that grew into an uproarious laugh. Yes, the giggling girl was Tillie, who was laughing so hard that she almost fell off her chair. This was the first time ever that Tillie laughed at herself; for a brief moment she saw some of her silly pride and foolish controlling ways, which were ridiculous indeed! The other students, including Willie, were most delighted at Tillie's hysterics. They were laughing and almost falling off their chairs, too. Miss Dullywinkle joined in the fun and celebrated by popping another Pillworth's Pepperminto Wintofrostimint in her mouth. Yes, Tillie was not mad but very glad; after all, she was quite proud of her brother. He had not only finished his report but had also turned an otherwise-dry research report into a fantastically interesting Heroical Storical that no one in Miss Dullywinkle's class would ever forget...Thanks to the Admiral and Captain, of course!

P.S. A most important postscript

I owe a debt of thanks to John Mack Faragher. Most of my understanding about Daniel Boone and the Battle of Boonesborough came from Faragher's excellent and well-researched book Daniel Boone, *The Life and Legend of an American Pioneer*. (Henry Holt and Company, Inc 1992) Faragher's research included the public record of the events of Boone's life, stories from those who were closest to Boone, friends, family and other contemporaries, and several stories from Boone himself of his adventures, including personal letters. Faragher writes:

> The record of Daniel Boone largely consists of the stories of humble

American men and women, written out laboriously with blunt pencils on scraps of paper, or told aloud in backwoods cabins or around campfires and taken down verbatim by antiquarian collectors. The materials for Boone's biography not only document the life of an American frontier hero, but reveal the thoughts and feelings of the diverse peoples of the frontier. The things people choose to say about Boone provide clues to their own concerns. Backcountry Americans celebrated Boone as one of their own. He was a hero, but a hero of a new, democratic type, a man who did not tower above the people but rather exemplified their longings and, yes, their limitations. "People may say what they please," as Simon Kenton put it, (Daniel Boone's friend) "but why do they say the things they do?"

Admiral Wright's Logbook of Researchorical Tips

Researchorical Tips - Very practical instructions in how to do an orderly, systematic investigation, into a field of knowledge to establish facts.

To be a knowledgeable shipmate, you must understand that no matter how smart or knowledgeable you are in a subject area, you still do not know very much compared to how much there is to know about everything. Remember, everyone only sees through a peephole.

Heroical-Storical-Observicorical-Researchorical-Scientifical-Mates are **researchers.** They carefully investigate a field of knowledge to discover what is fact and truth. They are also eager and enthusiastic learners. They are open and teachable and they are willing to *struggle to understand* whatever it is they need or want to know about.

A **researcher** is a collector of questions, ideas and facts.

What do you want to know? Suppose you have been asked to write a report about whales, those big blubbery belugas in the deep blue sea. You are excited to learn something new, but, like Willie, you can't stand the thought of having to write a **research** report.

Where do you start? You may have gone on a whale expedition and you can talk about what you learned from your experience. But you will likely need to get more information, and the place you can go to is the **library.**

But before you go to the library, take a few moments to think about your topic. Think about some questions you want to answer about your subject be it "big blubbery beluga whales," or something else. Remember, your **research** and report is as interesting as your questions. Asking good questions and finding good answers based on fact and reason build knowledge.

Note: You may need to read an article about your subject before you write down any questions. Getting an overview of your subject will help stimulate your thinking. Gaining some knowledge about a subject will help you ask more questions and that is a very good thing. Knowledge grows when questions are asked and reasonable answers are found.

Your **research** should be gathered from good sources of information. Here are some sources you can use.

Use your school and public libraries
Where to go to find what you need to know at the library

- Card catalogs—books, recordings, videos, etc.
- Computer catalogs—books, recordings, videos, etc.
- Encyclopedias—general information about a topic
- Magazine Guide—guide to magazine articles
- Reference Books—information on everything from ants to zebras

Talk to experts and professionals who might know something about your subject.

Ask your teacher, a parent or your friends about what they know.

Write your questions in a journal or on note cards.

FOR EXAMPLE:

Subject—Beluga Whales

Write one question per note card or page in a journal.

What are the physical characteristics of beluga whales?

· 100 feet long
· skin color is white
· weigh over 150 tons
· nearly hairless skin
· flipper-like forelimbs
· flat horizontal tail

On your note card or journal page, be sure to write down where you got your information. This is important; a good **researcher** always knows his or her sources for information about their subject of study.

After you have a notebook full of questions and answers about your subject then write your report.

But before you begin...

Make sure that you are following these important **RESEARCHORICAL** steps!

1. **Select your Subject**

Ask questions and more questions. Go from general to specific.

2. **Gather Information**

Find good sources of information. Use your library, the internet, experts, friends, family, magazine articles, videos, personal experience, etc.

- Answer your questions
- Use note cards or journals
- Verify and check your information
- Write down where you got your information

3. Link Your Ideas

Begin with an interesting hook, a story about your subject. Give a brief outline of what you are going to write about and be excited about your subject. A little enthusiasm goes a long way when you are reporting about something. If you are not interested or you do not care about your subject, do you think the reader of your report will be interested?

Organize your questions and answers into meaningful paragraphs and make sure your facts are accurate and that they flow and tie together.

Read your report aloud to yourself and then find a friend to read it to. Be sure that your report is interesting, well developed and makes good sense!

Use stories, quotes, pictures, and charts to add further detail and interest to your report.

End with a strong point that tells the reader something new that you discovered or learned about your subject that you did not know before.

4. Check Your Report

- Do you have clear, complete sentences?
- Are your paragraphs well organized?
- Do your ideas connect to each other?
- Have you covered your subject completely?
- Have you used quotation marks correctly?
- Did you check for spelling, grammar and punctuation?
- Is your report written neatly or typed correctly?

5. List your sources–Bibliography (You don't want to be guilty of plagiarism.)

BOOKS Author (last name first). Title. City where the book is published:Publisher, copyright date.

Fisher, Amy Beluga Whales. New York City: Oak Press, 1990

MAGAZINES Author (last name first). "Title of the article." Title of the magazine date (day month year): page numbers of the article.

Wing, Joseph. "Blubbery Friends" <u>Marine World</u> 8 July 1998:pg. 23-25

ENCYCLOPEDIAS "Article title." <u>Title of the reference book</u>. Edition (if known). Year published.

"Whales." <u>The World Book Encyclopedia.</u> 1995 ed.

FILMS, SLIDES, VIDEOTAPES Title. Medium (film, videocassette, etc.) Production company, date. Time length.

<u>Communication Systems among Beluga Whales</u> Video cassette. National Geographic 1998 30 minutes

INTERVIEWS Person you interviewed (last name first). Type of interview. Date.

Field, Erin. Personal Interview 16, September 1998

ON-LINE SOURCES (simplified entry) Author (last name first). "Title of article." Title of file year or date of publication. On-line, Name of computer network. Date of access. Available: electronic address.

Jones, Jeffrey. "Fascinating Belugas." <u>Under the Sea Quarterly</u> Apr.–June 1997. On-line. Internet. 11 September 1998. Available http://www.ppc.new.edu

Admiral Wright's
Dictionorical of
Heroical Storical Words

Absolutely Genuine Gold Stars—A special gold star given by Admiral Wright to Willie or Tillie when knowledge is understood and remembered about the facts and experience of a particular hero's life. The Admiral makes it clear that a gold star does not make Willie or Tillie more valuable, important or special because they have earned one. A gold star, according to the Admiral, "doesn't make you a better you because a 'you' is far more valuable than gold. A 'you' is a living, breathing being, made up of all sorts of special wonder!"

Admiral Wright—A British Admiral who is a wacky wonderfilled time traveler. He is an exciting storyteller, and can't wait to share "heroical storicals," intriguing stories about heroes from history. The Admiral discovers heroes on his world travels aboard the Shiny Shiny Silver Ship. He brings to homeport his mysterious trunk packed full with collectibles gathered during his adventurous quest for heroes.

Admiral Wright's Heroes Great Wall of Faith—A circular wall in Admiral Wright's Heroical Storical Laboratory. Displayed on the wall are framed pictures of distinguished characters, heroes from history. These heroes are framed because they stepped out in faith and believed the impossible in order to sacrifice and serve others.

Captain Perry Parrot—The beloved sidekick of Admiral Wright. Wacky, clumsy and quirky, the Captain is quick to add his bird's-eye view to the Admiral's grand pontifications. He is steadfast and loyal, the Admiral's first mate and true friend.

Character Champions—Heroes of the highest kind, indomitable individuals who possess the best and truest character. Such persons persevere and pursue honesty, integrity, faith, goodness and doing right. Champions like these have inspired countless generations to greater service and sacrifice for others.

Chief Blackfish—Daniel Boone's adopted "father," the leader of the Shawnees. He liked and respected Boone so much that he thought of Boone as "one of his own dear sons" and adopted Boone into his family.

Daniel Boone—One of the greatest frontiersmen who ever lived, he blazed the Wilderness Road and founded Boonesborough, Kentucky. Boone and his group successfully fought off an attack by the Shawnee on Boonesborough in 1779. Though Boone had many battles over land with native people, he had great respect for them. He acknowledged that he learned many of his frontier skills from the natives as a small boy growing up in the Pennsylvania woods. At the end of Boone's life, he said that "the Indians were some of the best friends he had ever known." Boone also wrote in a letter at the end of his life, "I always loved God ever since I could recollect." Draper Collection State Historical Society of Wisconsin.

Desk Fishing—The act of going into one's school desk and searching for special treasures during class time.

Divine Intervention—The action of the Sovereign Creator God in the affairs of humans.

Dullywinkle Doom—A miserable, cold, hard and shameful seat known as the dunce stool. Located in the front corner of Miss Dullywinkle's class. Students sit on it as punishment for misbehavior in class, such as desk fishing.

Extraordinary Black-Rimmed Glasses—Very special and unusual glasses that enable the wearer to see far more than they ever dreamed or imagined.

Faith Power—Faith in the Creator God who enables one to step out into the unknown and believe the impossible. Faith Power also enables one to believe the unbelievable, and see the invisible.

Gauntlet—A tribal custom, a kind of greeting put on for the entertainment and amusement of the tribes. If a prisoner was taken, a whole village—including the women and children—would stand in two parallel lines, with antlers, bats, poles, sticks and rocks to beat and injure the prisoner, who was made to run between the lines, from one end to the other.

Heroical Storical—An extremely intriguing story about an outstanding hero from history.

Heroical Storical Laboratory—A simply outrageously wonderful secret laboratory located deep under Admiral Wright's Ship Shop. The laboratory is in a large octagonal room and it is designed to look both like a scientific laboratory and a library. There are four telescopes positioned in four of the eight corners and in the other four corners microscopes sit on wooden tables. Floor to ceiling bookshelves fill half the room and they are arranged in a pattern like sections of an orange. A rug with a map of the solar system rests on the floor in the middle of the room. There is a high-backed chair and two round cushioned stools positioned in the center of the unusual rug. A strange hotchocolatematic gurgles in a far corner of the laboratory.

Heroical-Storical-Observicorical-Research-orical-Scientifical Mate—A character who likes to figure things out. Such a character asks questions to find reasonable answers and tries their best because they care about others and themselves. They also are very curious about heroes who are champions of good character that is the heroical part. The storical part has to do with an extremely intriguing story about the hero's outstanding deeds of courage and sacrifice. The observicorical part has to do with paying attention to the hero's storical and asking inquisitive questions. The researchorical part has to do with a close and careful examination of a hero's storical or any other subject or problem. The scientifical part has to do with a careful and orderly approach to the study of a hero's storical or anything else.

Hotchocolatematic—A very special hot chocolate machine. An odd contraption, almost the size of a refrigerator with pipes shooting out, some in wild loops and some pointing straight up. The machine is found in Admiral Wright's Heroical Storical Laboratory. It dispenses hot chocolate only on polite demand, with whipped cream and chocolate sprinkles. Its dispensing is a small wonder to behold as it pours out a warm mug of some of the best tasting hot chocolate with a grand display of gurgling and boiling noises as steam shoots out of its wild loops.

Knowledge Bank—A place in one's brain where facts are put. Deposits of knowledge, information and understanding about everything, are put into the brain. Knowledge from the brain bank is drawn out when needed to communicate interesting thoughts and ideas.

Master Desk Fisher—A student who has perfected his desk fishing skills to a degree that he will never ever be caught by the teacher during class time.

Mean Billy Bones—A nasty spitball-shooting student in Miss Dullywinkle's class, who makes Willie Venturely his target when Willie's sitting on the dunce stool.

Mind Wander—Occurs when a mind floats around from this to that and does not focus on what it is hearing and thinking about. It is a most unaware place to be in. The opposite of Mind Wander is Mind Focus where the individual disciplines their thoughts to pay attention to knowledge, (or whatever is going on around them). Knowledge is mostly gained from study and experience and the by-product of such an endeavor is that the mind learns and grows.

Miss Chatterberry—Willie and Tillie's nanny, a kindly white-haired woman who keeps the home and minds the twins (if she can) while their father works during the day.

Miss Dullywinkle—A well meaning and sincere fifth grade teacher who doesn't understand that not all students learn the same way. She has a passion for reading out of encyclopedias and popping Pillworth's Pepperminto Wintofrostimints into her mouth during oral readings about heroes from history.

Mrs. Dexter—A serious and attentive librarian who attempts to keep students, like Willie Venturely, who are undisciplined and unfocused, on the right path of discipline and order as they pursue research for class reports.

Pillworth's Pepperminto Wintofrostimint — A very special-tasting mint that is filled with peppermint and winterfrosty flavors. It is also Miss Dullywinkle's favorite mint that she enjoys during her oral encyclopedic readings about heroes from history.

Quantum Space Atomic Clock—Admiral Wright's clock that precisely counts the vibrations of atoms to measure the passing of time.

Researchorical Tips—Practical helps in how to do an orderly, systematic investigation, research in a field of knowledge to establish facts.

Richard Callaway—A frontiersman and contemporary of Daniel Boone and father-in-law of Jemima, Daniel's daughter. Callaway was known to be hotheaded and mean and the one who first appeared to start scuffling with the Shawnee warriors, right before the Battle began.

Rifle-Barreled Squirt Gun—The first known squirt gun invented by Daniel's brother, Squire. It was designed to put out the hard to reach fires in the corners of the fort during the Battle of Boonesborough.

S. S. Ship Shop—Admiral Wright's nautical store "where only the curious dare to venture." The shop, with its red door, is filled with all sorts of interesting curios and collectibles gathered from the many adventures of the Admiral and Captain.

Silly Ditty—A ridiculous and silly poem with rhyming words that tells something about someone or a thing or an abstract idea. A silly ditty is a favorite way for the Admiral and Captain to tell an important idea or moral lesson that Willie and Tillie need to be reminded of.

Shiny Shiny Silver Ship—Admiral Wright's very special flying silver ship. The sails of the ship are made of richly embroidered cloth that have gold and silver threads running every direction. They have a shimmering criss-crossed pattern that makes them appear electric. The base of the ship is made up of the shiniest metallic silver imaginable and it reflects light from all directions.

Tillie Venturely—The twin sister of Willie who can't stop herself from reminding her brother to pay attention and mind his lessons at school. Tillie learns there are other ways to learn than sitting at a desk and reading a book, thanks to the Admiral and Captain.

Willie Venturely—A very adventurous and curious boy who can't stand Miss Dullywinkle's history class and avoids his bothersome twin sister whenever possible. One of Willie's favorite activities is desk fishing during Miss

Dullywinkle's readings about characters from history.

William Hancock—A contemporary of Daniel Boone who helped defend Boonesborough. He also had been captured by the Shawnee at the same time that Daniel was. He escaped from Chillicothe on foot in the middle of the night in his very natural self. Hancock wrongly accused Boone of being a traitor who had promised to help the Shawnee win Boonesborough.

Very Yellow Plastic Pocket Protectors—A yellow plastic insert that slips inside the pocket of a lab coat. It is designed to serve the purpose of preventing unsightly ink marks on fresh new lab coat pockets. Admiral Wright values such a tool greatly and it is part of the official uniform of the Heroical-Storical-Observicorical-Researchorical-Scientifical-Mate.

Do you like the
Heroical Storicals Series?
Visit our Heroical Storical Web site at

www.heroicalstoricals.com

Take a sneak peak of the new Heroical Storical on *Harriet Tubman and the Underground Railroad*, due out soon.

You won't be bored or disappointed on this web site. Lots of fun-filled activities, interesting facts, maps, cool links and much, much more await you...

Send in your hero stories about yourself or someone you know, or learned about, who did an outstanding deed or act of kindness showing sacrifice and courage. Such good deeds deserve a rightful place on Admiral Wright's Character Champion Banner. The power of a good deed always shines brighter than the blackest night!"

The hero's story and name will be written on Admiral Wright's Character Champion Banner! Very cool indeed!

Book Two
Harriet Tubman and the
Underground Railroad

Harriet Tubman (1820-1913). A courageous black American woman who was a slave until she escaped in 1849 and became one of the most successful conductors on the UNDERGROUND RAILROAD. The "railroad" was a loosely organized system for helping runaway slaves escape to freedom. Harriet led more than 300 slaves to freedom by traveling at night, staying in "safe houses" and risking her life many times.

Join Willie and Tillie on an exciting, fun-filled and at times danger-filled adventure as they meet up again with the Admiral and Captain and find themselves whisked back in time to the pre-civil war slave days where they learn a lesson or two about courage from their new friend Harriet Tubman.

About the Author

Annie Winston, a graduate of UC Berkeley, a schoolteacher and single mom of three children, wrote Admiral Wright's Heroical Storicals late at night and into the wee morning hours. Annie comments, "I had to write something interesting and fun, otherwise I would have fallen asleep!"

About the Cover Illustrator

Mark Fredrickson is a nationally renowned illustrator. He has won the Society of Illustrator's Gold Medal as well as many other awards of distinction. Fredrickson's client list includes Time Warner, Universal Studios, Random House and Levi Strauss.

About the Inside Illustrator

Keith Locke's previous client list includes Universal Studios, Dreamworks SKG, Focus on the Family, the George W. Bush administration, Outreach Marketing, Coca-Cola, Pepsi-Cola, Penguin Putnam books and various others.

Shipnotes

Shipnotes

Shipnotes

Shipnotes

Shipnotes

Shipnotes

Shipnotes

Shipnotes

